# An
# END
## OF
# TROUBLES

An Anthology from
History Through Fiction

ISBNs: 978-1-963452-16-7 (pb);
978-1-963452-17-4 (eBook)
Book Cover Design: Mel Nigro, melnigro.com
Interior Book Design: Inanna Arthen, inannaarthen.com
Library of Congress Control Number: 2024952045
First Printing: 2025
Printed in the United States of America

# CONTENTS

# MRS. PRICE

❧

## *Jeanine Boulay*

Shirley and Joe Price sat on their stoop, he on the top step and she one below, her legs outstretched on the concrete slab. He picked his guitar. She watched him—watched the fingers of his right hand moving across the strings, watched the fingers of his left pressing down on them at the neck, hard, keeping each in place for the beat or two he needed at a chord before securing the next the same way, watched the cigarette loose at his lips arch upward each time he hummed along. It was early November and the midday sun was out and falling over everything; the sidewalk, the brick of the buildings, the brims of men's hats as they passed. Its warmth and light had the effect of whitewashing the landscape, and one could almost forget it was noon on a Monday. Joe rested his cigarette on the stoop and leaned down to her, strumming with new purpose.

"They used to tell me I was building a dream, with peace and glory ahead, why should I be standing in line, just waiting for bread?" He hummed through the next parts, stopping only for the refrain, "Brother can you spare a dime?" Then he clapped the front of the guitar into silence and caught her eye before changing his tune.

"Old King Cole was a merry old soul, and a merry old soul was he," he sang. "He called for his pipe and he called for his bowl and he called for his fiddlers three." He paused, leaned in further.

"My mommy said if I was good she'd send me to the store," he sang. "She said she'd make some gingerbread if I would sweep the floor…" They were face to face, the guitar between their bodies.

"Glory glory hallelujah, teacher hit me with a ruler…"

Shirley slapped his leg. He let the guitar fall across his lap and took a drag of his cigarette, smirking.

"I know all the kids' songs," Joe said. "I could sing them to our boy. Or girl," he winked.

"Again with this?" She rolled her head back and looked at the sky. "It's such a beautiful day, Joe. Don't start with this again."

When they first married, she'd put him off because, she said, she wanted him for herself before having to share. Which was partly true. Except that sharing in this case meant the uneven divide between nursing, diapers, and crying, and anything that might make up the rest of her. Now, she put him off for practical reasons, like breadlines. But it was getting difficult. In bed, when the calendar read her risky days, she urged him away from her at the end, pushing his hips with her hands. Still, he'd whisper and place his face in her neck, keeping her close. Her friend Helen told her about the newest thing, latex, that she and her husband had started to use, but Shirley doubted Joe would go for it. At least sharing a room with her grandmother at night served as some excuse, although Joe swore the old woman was deaf and they heard her snores as early as seven each night. Her parents must maneuver the same situation sharing with her younger sister, but that was a thought she needn't dwell on.

"We're six mouths already. Who's going to share their potatoes and peas with a seventh?"

"A baby doesn't need potatoes and peas! He'll have you," he said, reaching over and squeezing her breast. "And this, depression—or whatever they're calling it—is going to break by the time he's old enough for real food."

Shirley rolled her eyes, made a V shape with her fingers

and extended them towards his cigarette. He glanced both directions of the sidewalk for passersby before handing it to her. She took a long drag and exhaled, then laid her head on his thigh beside the neck of the guitar. He lifted it and began strumming again, his fingers light on the strings. A man rounded the corner, his overcoat unbuttoned and swinging at his calves. He shot a couple squinty-eyed looks at them before hollering, "Shut up!" as he passed. He kicked a trash can a few steps beyond them and threw his fedora at the sidewalk. They heard his mutters the length of his walk down the block.

"I'm glad you took a break today," Shirley said. "It's too nice out to be feeling like that."

On Tuesday, they resumed the work of looking for work. Joe went back to the line at City Hall. Shirley took the train up to Ninth Avenue, where Helen had told her some of the garment factories were taking girls. Men pushed racks of dresses and coats down the street and over sidewalks, creating narrow spaces for pedestrians. She weaved through them, dodging herds of towering headless bodies as they barreled toward her. She found a short line gathered outside a gray concrete building and stepped into it, gauging her place from the entrance before inquiring as to the establishment.

"Are they looking for girls?" she asked the woman at the end of the line.

"That's what I hear," the woman said, barely turning her head to reply.

The line moved. Shirley made note of each person as they went in, and whether or not they came back out. If you were looking for work, you worked. If you came out, it was because you were turned away. There were a few men who dotted the line between the gathered women; each exited almost as soon as he'd entered.

"Like they can sew," the woman ahead of her mumbled.

Three Negro girls were waiting together. Friends, chatting about the dresses they saw roll by as they stepped closer to the wide glass doors. They came out as a group. Shirley understood why the woman in front of her had little interest in talking. You had a better chance at a place if it was clear you were on your own. Of course, you had a better chance if you were white, too. But white women were being turned away more often than Shirley expected. Were they too old? Unable to sew? (Was there a test?) Couldn't they speak English? She looked for the differences between her and each of them as they walked into the street. She smoothed the pockets of her overcoat and pushed on her cheeks. Lifting her chin, she pulled on the heavy glass.

A table was set up in the hallway. Three men were spaced out in seats behind it, clipboards set in front of them. Two were already speaking to hopeful prospects, so she approached the third. It was unclear where the hallway led but she could hear the beats of sewing machines above her head.

"Name?"

"Shirley Price."

"Age?"

"Twenty-two."

"Married?"

"Yes."

"Husband's occupation?"

"He's currently looking."

"Unemployed?" The man looked up at her for the first time. He wasn't very old.

"He's actually down at City Hall right now. They say there are work assignments there. I'm sure he'll have something by the end of the day."

"I understand, Miss," he said.

"Mrs."

"Yes, I understand. Come back to us when your husband is working."

"Sir?"

"Let's get your husband working. Then maybe we can help you," he said. "Thank you." He began writing on his clipboard as a sign that the interview was over.

⁂

That night, her grandmother's throaty snorts in the background, she told Joe. They sat on a mattress on the floor, their backs against the wall. Her legs were tangled with his beneath the quilt her mother had sewn as their wedding gift (she was the real talent).

"Three times today. And not the first time I've heard it," she said. His hand was on her back, his fingers tapping out a rhythm.

"It's admirable, at least," he said.

"Admirable?"

"The respect for a man's pride, that's all."

"Joe, my parents can't keep us this way. The money's running out. We need to contribute."

"We all need to contribute, Shirley. You see it out there. What is there to do?" He stopped tapping on her back, let his hand rest there. "It'd be better if we weren't married. That's what you're telling me."

"Joe…"

They sat quiet together, each looking off to separate corners of the floor.

"What about that? What if we pretended we weren't married? What if the answer to that interview question was 'no'?"

"Joe."

"Buck the system."

"You can't lie to an employer," she said. "We'd end up fired as soon as we got the work."

"We could really fake it. I could go stay with my cousin,

Hardy. What's another body on the floor at night?" They were deep into fantasy now.

"My mother would die under a lie like that," she said.

"We wouldn't tell her. We'd really fake it," he said. "But do you think she'd let me take the quilt?" She elbowed him, laughing. Then she sighed.

"Let's sleep. I can't even think about this." She uncrossed her legs from his and slid down the wall until she was flat on the mattress. "I wish it were yesterday again," she said.

"I wish it were tomorrow's tomorrow."

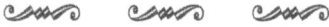

∽ ∽ ∽

They made their plan. Over the next week, the mattress beneath them, they crafted their lie, their reasons for separating, the way they'd reveal their prank to friends and family once this hard stretch was over and they reunited. In whispers, Joe glossed over their time apart and talked about later—later with money. He described a little basement apartment in Chelsea, a two bedroom. There was a refrigerator with bacon and beer. There was a nursery, there was a stool in the corner where he perched and played guitar while Shirley nursed.

She was most surprised by her family's lack of surprise. They accepted the news as an inevitable outcome and warmly wished Joe well on the afternoon he left, duffle bag slung over one shoulder, guitar strap over the other. Her father muttered a comment about a useless musician, but declined to repeat it when she feigned she hadn't heard him. She was least surprised by how quickly she found herself sitting at one of several rows of long tables lined with Singers and spools.

Each morning she wiped her machine down with a loose piece of cloth, comforted by its black shine. She kept her fingers tense as she pushed the fabric through, the stitches reverberating through the tops of her hands. There were women sitting at each of her elbows, and women at their elbows, down the line the length of the factory's wall. They sat in wooden chairs just like the ones at her kitchen table, with rounded top rails and thin splats at their backs; enough to cradle their bodies when they leaned backwards, but not enough to cushion them. The sound was raucous; a constant hum and thump that made her feel like her heart was racing away at a pace she'd never catch. She took that sound home with her at night, felt its rush in her dreams.

"Shirley," her elbow mate called over the beats. "Shirley!"

She took a small balled up square of fabric out of her ear, a trick she'd learned from one of the older women, and leaned over to hear.

"I have something for us," she said, "for break." She gave a wink.

When the bells rang twenty minutes later, the two girls found their way to the alley behind the building and stood in a corner, surrounded by cement. Jean pulled a cigarette and matchbox out of her apron pocket.

"So, you've been with us for a couple of months now. Did you decide? Are you going to be a union girl?" Jean asked, before lighting the cigarette she held between her lips.

"I don't know. I guess so. I just don't want to be a part of any strikes. I need this work. We all need this work."

"Mmmmm," Jean blew smoke out of her nose in agreement. "But look what you had to do to get this work." She was the only friend at the factory who knew Shirley's secret. "Anyway, the good stuff makes it worth it, the classes and whatnot. They've even started talking about putting on a musical."

"A musical?" Shirley took the cigarette between her fingers.

"Yes. You play an instrument? Sing?"

"No, not me," she said. Joe.

"Well, I bet they'll teach you. Anyway, you should come see about it. I'm going tonight."

"Do you sing?"

"I'm not bad in the shower. Besides, there's bound to be some men around, directing, producing, whatnot. They'll need

11

a male lead for a show. As much as I love all of you ladies, us single girls need to meet a boy somewhere, right?" Jean winked.

"I can't tonight," Shirley said. "Next time."

At the end of the work day, Shirley walked from the factory to Eisenberg's on Fifth Avenue to buy dinner for her date with Joe. They had been meeting in Madison Square Park since he left her home, and Shirley always brought food. Joe would accept it if they ate together on a park bench, but would not join her inside a shop if it meant she would be paying the bill. But she knew he was hungry; he still had not found work. She ordered one slice of liver loaf and a mayonnaise sandwich, and watched the man behind the counter tear sheets of greasy wax paper and wrap the items with speed and precision.

They would sit and eat sheepishly, keeping their meal tucked in paper as best they could, hiding it from the hungry eyes of passersby. Once, Shirley gave half an egg sandwich to a child who lingered near them, which prompted Joe to comment on her maternal instincts. That time, he convinced her to go to Hardy's with him, and after whispering with his cousin, they were left alone in the back bedroom. He swore their baby would come from that tryst, and in the weeks that passed would even lay on her lap in the park and sing songs to her stomach. But by now she knew there was no baby coming, and she recognized relief in his expression when she told him so. Mostly, on these dates in the park, she would chatter about her days at the factory; the noise of the machines, the dresses she was making and mending, Jean. She spoke at a clip, filling up space so that Joe didn't need to share the details of his days. Rather than talk, he played his guitar. He strummed low chords with closed eyes, his face raised to the sky. He was somewhere else then.

She arrived at their bench with the brown bag under her arm. She liked this spot, across from the MetLife building, its looming clock tower and the scaffolded construction that was slowly creeping to meet it. She saw there in the sky, a goal; work, a raising up, a passage of time, tomorrow. Joe sat down. He smiled and held out his own brown bag.

"What's this?" she asked, surprised.

"A sweet," he said. "For my—" and he touched his finger to the tip of her nose.

"You shouldn't have, Joe." She didn't ask how he'd managed a purchase from a bakery.

They ate, passing the loaf and sandwich between them. Joe beamed when he broke the cookie in two. He watched her eat her half and then offered his. She knew to accept it. It wasn't until after their meal that she noticed.

"Joe," she paused. "Where is your guitar?"

"Oh, you know…"

"Joe."

"I needed to give Hardy some money if I wanted to stay. He's going to lose the place if he doesn't pay rent."

"You're not taking any space! You're on the floor!"

"There are a lot of guys that need a floor right now, Shirley. Guys coming and going from all over. And they're willing to pay a little something for it."

"You're his cousin!"

"It's just how it is," Joe said. He strummed his fingers on the bench.

"You sold your guitar," she said. "Joe."

He closed his eyes and lifted his chin, still playing the wood of the bench. She watched him for a moment, then turned back to her view of rising buildings. They sat together, their stomachs full.

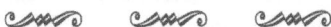

❧ ❧ ❧

The next week she went with Jean down to Waverly Place to see the rehearsal for the musical. The ladies' garment union banner hung from the arched stone entryway with "ILGWU" printed in red block letters, and she lingered in the vestibule to take in the photographs that lined the walls. One, marked 1910, showed four women standing side by side, each wearing a wide-brimmed hat with feathers and velvet bows. The layers of their long dresses and coats were covered by wide sashes that read, "Picket / Ladies / Tailors / Strikers." Shirley looked into their faces and tried to identify the emotion behind the expressions she saw there; smirks filled with anger, purpose, pride, pomposity, delight. There was a framed front page of The New York Times with the headline, "Heroic Young Forewoman Loses Her Life to Save Others from Death in Flames," above photos of women who perished in the 1911 Triangle Shirtwaist Fire, each face printed as though framed in an oval locket that hung around some mother's neck. Another was of a group huddled for a photo from the center of their work room, squeezed between rows of sewing machines and reams of cloth. They could have been her friends from the factory, smiling at the camera with closed lips, hands on each other's shoulders. They wore their own buttoned up shirtwaists, some with cuffed sleeves or thin black ties knotted and hanging from their necks. Their vested foreman stood in the middle. As she moved through the doors to the main hall, she passed the large gold framed photo of a man with salt and pepper hair, the triangle of his widow's peak marking his forehead. The attached gold plaque read, "President of the International Ladies' Garment Workers' Union." Even here, she thought, men were at the center of everything.

The hall inside was filled with groups of people, their voices echoing through the open space. Jean spotted her and waved her over to the group she stood with, several women and one man whom she had positioned herself next to.

"This is Shirley, my newest recruit," Jean said. The group gave nods and smiles.

"Shirley. Don Peters," the man said, extending his hand. "Choral Director. We were just about to run through a number.

Listen and jump in where you like." To the group he said, "Two, three, four:

"Sing me a song with social significance
Or you can sing 'til you're blue
Let meaning shine from ev'ry line
Or I won't love you.
Sing me of wars and sing me of breadlines
Tell me of front page news
Sing me of strikes and last minute headlines
Dress your observation in syncopation!
Sing me a song with social significance
There's nothing else that will do
It must get hot with what is what
Or I won't love you."

Shirley joined in for the chorus on the second round and when they finished Jean exclaimed, "You can sing!"

"A little," she blushed.

"Auditions are tonight," Don said.

"Oh, I don't think so," she said. "What is it, even?"

"It's called Pins and Needles."

"Pins and Needles?" she asked. "So, it's us?" She glanced around at the circle of women.

"Yes! You've got it!" He seemed satisfied. "The idea is for it to be a show of the times, a rotating cast of real garment workers starring on stage, songs about current issues, real theater about real life!"

Shirley watched the auditions from a row of folding chairs set up in front of a makeshift stage. But on their walk home, Jean urged her to continue coming to rehearsals.

"I had no idea you had a voice like that."

"I haven't shared much. It was—" Joe that was the real talent. But suddenly she didn't want to name him. She didn't have space for him in the world she had stepped into tonight. She thought of their park bench and talking to him about the hall, the bustle, the music and enthusiasm; but she couldn't imagine the words coming out at all. "It was always someone else's dream," she said.

"You could start with lessons," Jean said. "The union offers them over at the High School."

"The High School?"

"Washington Irving. Up Broadway at 16th Street. That's where they do the Workers' University courses."

"University…" Shirley repeated, as they walked past empty storefronts.

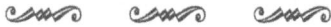

∽  ∽  ∽

They'd eaten pastrami, as a treat. She thought it might soften their talk, if she were to tell Joe about the musical. But she hadn't mentioned it yet. Each time she thought to start— You would have loved the songs—she felt as if a shield were in front of her body, and the words would not pass through had she said them. Joe also was quiet. She realized she did not know if it was reticence on his part, or anger, or simply the absence of the guitar that had always filled the space between them.

"I have some news, Shirley," he said.

"You found work?" Her mood broke into joy.

"Yes—"

"That's wonderful!" She reached for his hands.

"It's upstate."

"Upstate?"

"Near Buffalo. I'm joining the CCC. Going up there to plant trees."

"The reforestation program? Through the government?"

"I can get in with Hardy. His family's on relief, and they count me as one of them since my parents died. Glad my father's not here to see this, his son taking a hand-out."

"Joe."

"And I'm a young unmarried man. Just the kind they're looking for." He looked in her eyes.

"Joe."

They spent another hour on the bench, leaning against one another, planning. Joe knew a few details; he and Hardy would be at a camp together, they could each pack one trunk, they'd likely be clearing trails and making parks out of the forests bordering Pennsylvania. The stories he'd heard made the life out to be all right, with boys getting baseball teams together and playing music combos. He was going to try and get his guitar back to bring with him. He thought some fresh air might do him good. He promised to write letters each week, and reading them would feel just like this, just like being in the park together. This time, he didn't speak of an apartment in Chelsea.

In the bedroom with her grandmother that night, Shirley lay in the center of the mattress, eyes on the ceiling. She thought back to their wedding day. She had worn the best dress in her closet, the pink one with cap sleeves and front buttons. They took pictures on the small stretch of lawn behind her parents' brownstone and danced to a song Joe had put on the record player. He sang to her, "I can't give you anything but love, that's the only thing I've plenty of," his lips moving alongside her temple like kisses. Her father poured punch and gave a toast to their growing family. Shirley closed her eyes and placed her palms over her pelvis. She fell asleep waiting for tears that didn't come.

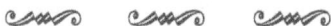

⁓  ⁓  ⁓

It took a year and a half for a cast of union girls to be ready to show Pins and Needles. Jean made it into a supporting chorus role. Shirley held back, but went with Jean to every rehearsal and ended up working on costumes as a seamstress. The girls worked their days at the factories, and spent their evenings and weekends at the Labor Stage, a theater the ILGWU had leased and renamed. Even from backstage, Shirley learned all of the numbers. On the line during the day, when she was certain her voice would be drowned out by the roar and thump of the sewing machines, she would sing. The hum in her chest matched the reverberation around her then, and she felt aligned, rather than outrun. On her lunch breaks, she would walk down Thirty-Ninth Street and sit at a bus stop across from the Labor Stage, which everyone still called the old Princess Theater, looking up at it as she used to with the MetLife building.

Except that the old Princess Theater was nothing much to look at from the outside. It might have been an office building, with its flat facade and windows, but for the simple marquee hung over its doors. But Shirley liked sitting across from its plainness and knowing the secrets offered inside; the French tapestries that hung from its walls, the carved ceilings and banisters, the elegant theater boxes built off the arch from which there wasn't a poor view of the house. And the secret world that existed inside, where the women of her daily life became larger than life, their stories and voices amplified by the very walls.

There was the other secret she thought of during her lunch breaks, the one of her marriage that she continued to keep. But it was fading from her, both in how close Joe felt to her world, and in how close she wanted him to feel. His letters had slowed, first coming weekly as promised, then monthly, and now, rarely. He had formed a musical group and they played often in the town closest to camp, where they held dances for the CCC boys to attend. Shirley understood the unsaid part of these letters, the girls from town that also attended the dances, that swooned at performances, that were there to lean against Joe as he strummed his guitar. Of course, that had been her. She'd been drawn to Joe's musicality, his talent. When they first met, she'd fantasized about them performing together, though she never revealed to him that she sang. At first she was self-conscious, then hesitant to take from his spotlight, his pride. She knew how special his talent made him feel, and also knew he couldn't stand to be minimized by her—I can do that, too—then, ultimately, she was eclipsed by him and stopped considering her place beside him and his guitar as anything more than audience member, admirer.

# MRS. PRICE

On Thursday nights she didn't go to rehearsal. Instead, she went over to Washington Irving. She took back to back classes, one on political philosophy and one on drama. There was money behind this show now, and professionals, and the ILGWU continued to talk up the plan to have a rotating cast of real life garment workers. Jean told her the directors already discussed taking the show on tour. Shirley had never left Manhattan. She didn't have the raw confidence that Jean possessed, or Joe. She knew if she was going to be a part of Pins and Needles, if she was going to reach for something beyond the Singer she faced every day, she needed to prepare.

On opening night, Shirley slipped away from the din of costumes and scene checks to her favorite perch across the street. She took in the invite-only crowd, dressed in their theater clothes. She was struck by the thought that this group, at least, did not appear to have had their dreams stolen by this "Great Depression," as it was now named. She considered the last few years, thought of dancing with Joe in her pink dress, her father's toast. Of lying in bed and saying goodbye. She thought of all the ways she had paid the price for this moment outside of the theater. And yet she felt—spared. No baby to care for, no husband to tend, no ring that marked her an old married woman. She approached the theater entrance along with the crowd, under the marquee that read Pins and Needles. One of the windows displayed a poster with the names of the writer and director, and some of the actors and their roles. Printed there were the names of her friends, some from her own work room, some she'd met through the union and rehearsals. Women that had come together, were forced together, had gained something, had made something new. She imagined her name on a poster like this one, assigned to a singing role, hanging in a theater window in Philadelphia or Boston. A lump hardened in her throat at the thought of the letters spelling out her name.

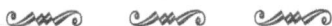

❧   ❧   ❧

On the Monday after the show, Shirley arranged with her factory manager to arrive late the next day. And so it was a Tuesday in November that she stood in line at City Hall. She found her way to the correct office and to a clerk who explained the process.

"And your reason?" the clerk asked her.

"Reason? I'm not sure—"

"Adultery? Abandonment? Abuse?" Shirley winced.

"A-Abandonment, I suppose." She lifted her chin, firming her body into the lie. "Yes, he left."

"All right," the clerk looked up briefly, "I'm sorry." He continued to explain how she would proceed in filing for divorce.

"And how, when, do I change my name?" Shirley interjected.

"Legally, when it's finalized. But many women just start using their maiden names as they go about their business." Their eyes met and she nodded.

As she gathered her belongings to leave she looked at him once more with gratitude.

"Thank you," she said.

"You're welcome, Ms.—?"

"Davis. Shirley Davis." In lights.

## THE END

## *About the Author*

Jeanine Boulay is a poet, fiction writer, and educator. A five-time New York Public Library Cullman Center for Teachers Fellow and three-time Academy for Teachers Fellow, Boulay has studied under Uwem Akpan, Ian Frazier, Karen Russell, and others while developing "Mrs. Price" and other stories in her recently completed collection. Boulay's short stories examine how women navigate historically significant moments of American life, while exploring how personal transformation intersects with social change. A Brooklyn educator for twenty years, Boulay now serves as a school administrator and lives in Princeton, Massachusetts, with her husband, two energetic boys, and their pet axolotl.

# THOSE BEREAVED

## *Candace Simar*

My only solace was to wander in the darkness, night after night, following the fence line around the prairie farm like a sleepwalker in the moonlight.

My hair hung witchy down my back. Dew wet my bare feet and turned the hem of my nightdress into a sodden mess that tangled my legs.

Neighbors had repaired the fence where it happened, but the churned ground marked the spot. An accident, everyone said. It could have happened to anyone, they said. But it hadn't happened to anyone. It happened to Jess. The bull hooked him in his belly and tossed him over the fence like a pile of rags. The wound proved mortal, a slow and painful agony.

Jess, still dying, urged prudence. The bull was valuable, he said, and we could ill afford the loss. But I insisted someone shoot the devil, or I would do it myself. A neighbor obliged, but I refused the meat. I'd starve first.

An owl's hoot echoed from the cottonwoods by the river. I cupped my hands around my mouth, and hooted back with a voice rusty from disuse. How many days had it been since I had spoken? I had become an old woman, though not yet twenty years old.

Two crosses stood at the family cemetery. The smaller read *Baby Brandt 1887*. The pain from last year etched my heart as surely as the carving on the marker. The old doctor woman said that I did nothing wrong, that babies died, and there was no remedy for it. Her words had not consoled me then, nor would I ever be consoled.

The other marker felt smooth beneath my fingers. Strange how everyone went on with their lives, though Jess was dead, and my world shattered. Someday, I would carve *Jess Brandt 1860-1888*, but not yet. Carving the letters made it real.

I stepped in a patch of porcupine grass on my way to the river. The Mad Dog was low this time of year, and I dangled my sore foot in the lazy water. How easy it would be to lie down and breathe in the coolness until my world ended. I edged away, not trusting myself.

Folks urged me to sell the farm and return to Wisconsin, but Mama was dead and the thought of Pa's new wife made my teeth hurt. Pa might come, especially if he thought he would profit from Jess's labors, but I would not allow that woman to set foot in my house. My brother had three years left in Yuma Prison, innocent or not. I had no one else.

I wouldn't tell the homefolks about Jess. At least not yet.

A sliver of pink showed in the east. I stumbled to my bed and slept like a stone.

"Verdie! Verdie Brandt!"

I scrambled awake, pushed back my hair, and peeked out the window, shielding my eyes with my hand against the light. Midday, and I was still abed. Bossy bellowed to be milked.

It was the old doctor woman astride her pony. Doctor Gamla carried a large bundle before her, and a valise tied to the saddle. She was not a real doctor, but someone everyone depended upon, just the same. The pony strained under the burden and sniffed the water trough.

The old lady hunched in the saddle. Blue eyes sparked like sapphires from deep wrinkles.

Her black widow's weeds carried a greenish tinge that did not suit her. I should be wearing black. The thought startled me, and I looked down at my muddy nightdress and dirty feet, ashamed of my poor showing.

"Hello, Verdie." Doctor Gamla pointed her chin toward the bundle on her lap. "I bring you a cure."

I wasn't sick.

She lifted the bundle and held it out to me. "Careful, now."

I took it, wary of the pony's teeth. The bundle knobbed all elbows and knees, and felt light as a baby bird. Inside I discovered a girl about three years old. A blue ribbon tied wayward curls and a gold locket hung around her neck. She looked at me without a sound, not even a whimper.

"Who is she?"

"A foundling." Doctor Gamla climbed down and loosed the valise. "They were on the train when her mother's pains started. They called me from the Nickelbo Depot, but too late." I set the girl down as if she were made of glass. She stood without making a single peep.

"She died?" I whispered lest I distress the girl.

"She bled out. I couldn't have done anything, but might have learned the girl's name and how to contact her people."

"What's your name?" I knelt to speak to her eye to eye. The girl's face remained expressionless. She stuck two fingers in her mouth.

Doctor Gamla was little more than rag and bone herself. She hefted the valise and started into the house. I took the girl's hand and followed.

Doctor Gamla plopped the valise down with a sigh. "Why a woman would go galivanting so close to her time is beyond foolishness."

I saw my house through Doctor Gamla's eyes: the crumbs on the table, the unmade bed, and the overflowing ashes in the stove. The air breathed sour and stale.

"I'm feeling peckish," Doctor Gamla said. "Who knows when the girl last ate."

"Sit," I said "I'll fix something."

Doctor Gamla perched on a chair and rocked forward and back. When I looked again, she sat with her chin on her chest. Her breath whistled. A dipper of water, a jar of milk, and a half loaf of stale bread was all I could offer. She roused with the clatter of crockery.

The girl made no move to eat. I sprinkled sugar over the sopped bread, and held the spoon to her mouth. She turned and clamped her lips. I managed to get a few swallows of milk into her, but not a single bite.

"We don't know what to do with her," Doctor Gamla said. "I thought you could keep her for a while."

"Oh no." My brain clouded with fog as it had since Jess's death. "I couldn't—"

"You can. It's only decent." A glob of milk settled into a crease beside her mouth.

"You're not doing anything else."

Doctor Gamla was famous for bluntness, but I was in no state to care for a child, and I told her so.

"Bertha Walvatne is about to deliver." Her face looked gray and drawn. Someone should be fetching and doing for Doctor Gamla, at her age. I realized she waited for an answer.

The girl's eyelids drooped. "Just tonight," I said. "No longer."

"All right," Doctor Gamla said with a sniff. "My cures work if you can stand them." She asked me to investigate the valise. "Maybe you'll find information about her people."

I carried the girl to my bed. Her petticoats were embroidered with fine stitches. While the girl slept, I donned a black dress, and milked poor Bossy. I tidied the kitchen, swept the hearth, and cleared the ashes. Then I stoked the fire and stirred a batch of cornbread. The girl had to eat.

I tiptoed to the bed and discovered the girl's eyes were open.

"Come," I said. "Let's feed the chickens."

I helped her to her feet, but she stood in bewilderment.

I took her hand, and she followed as if in a trance. Like how I wandered at night. A tenderness rose up and I struggled to squelch the feeling. I couldn't get attached.

Bossy lumbered toward the pasture. The cat mewed over new kittens. The girl didn't smile. She walked only if led.

At supper I tried to spoon corn bread with fresh butter into her mouth. She turned away. "You have to eat." I forced a spoon into her mouth and she swallowed. A tear slipped down her cheek.

Later, I read to her from an old storybook, and tucked her into my bed for the night. I was responsible, and didn't like it. Walking was my only comfort.

Inside the valise was clothing for the girl, a woman's dress and nightgown, bloomers, stockings, a camisole, apron, hairbrush, comb, and tooth brush. A bundle of letters were wrapped in the *Montana Matrimonial News.* An advert, circled in pencil, caught my eye: *Widowman with small children seeks widow-woman in similar condition. Life has dealt cruel blows and our hearts are broken. My children need a mother and yours a father. Let's start over together. I like music. Julius Dahlen, Jamestown, Dakota Territory.*

I lit the lamp and sat down to read the letters addressed to Mrs. Ingrid Stenson of Moorhead, Minnesota. So, the girl's last name was Stenson. I felt like a peeping Tom. The first letter introduced Julius Dahlen. His handwriting was not of an educated man. He said his wife had died in childbed the previous winter. He could not manage the farm while caring for two boys. Like all farmers, he was land rich and cash poor. He lived in a sod house. He was honest, a hard worker, and a church-goer.

The next letter expressed sympathy for her husband's death. He agreed an asylum was no place for a well-behaved child, no matter what people said. Alice would thrive with brothers and speak when she was ready. His boys were loud enough for all of them. He once sang in the church choir. Now the boys demanded his attention.

Alice. The girl's name was Alice Stenson. She was an orphan without mention of kinfolk. Other letters described livestock, crops, and garden. His boys were getting wild without a mother. He thanked her for the tintype and apologized for having none to return. "Will you marry me without seeing a likeness?" He enclosed a letter of reference from the minister. "We cannot expect to love each other, but perhaps our union would benefit our children."

The minister claimed that Julius Dahlen was a man of fine moral character. He and his wife and boys had been a blessing to all who knew them. I rifled through the rest of the letters.

All spoke of grief and the need for a wife. "I do not expect you to love me. You and Alice can share a bed as long as you wish."

I felt my cheeks flush. A marriage of convenience. No wonder Ingrid Stenson did not demand a likeness.

The last letter mentioned railroad tickets. If they married before the birth, he would be the baby's legal father. She must send the trunk ahead so that it would arrive in time. The boys were jubilant about a new sister and mother. He would meet her at the depot. They would enter Holy Matrimony before heading out to the farm.

I stared out the window for a long time before crawling into bed beside Alice. Heat radiated from her little body.

I was almost asleep when I remembered Julius Dahlen. The poor man must be waiting at the depot. It was only right that he knew what happened. I rummaged for paper and quill. I asked him to return Alice's trunk on the next train.

The next morning, Doctor Gamla came while I was setting the bread sponge. She dipped a sugar lump into her cup of coffee and popped it into her mouth. I reported what I had discovered.

"Alice doesn't speak." I glanced over to where she sat on the front steps.

"She'll go to the asylum for the feeble minded, then," Doctor Gamla said. "Unlikely anyone will take her."

A lump rose in my throat and tears pushed behind my eyes. Julius Dahlen was right. An asylum was no place for a well-behaved girl. "She can stay, at least until Mr. Dahlen returns her trunk."

"So, you like my cure." Doctor Gamla's eyes flashed.

"She can stay longer," I said. "That's all. What about the funeral?"

"Need to locate kin before burial."

She agreed to post the letter. The train traveled to Jamestown once a day. The old woman, nimble for her years, climbed on her pony, and rode away. Alice ate a boiled egg, opening her mouth like a baby robin. Her appetite brightened my day.

Alice took my hand when it was time to do chores. My throat ached. That night, I kissed her. She sighed and snuggled into my shoulder. The next day, Alice reached toward a kitten. She was a sweet girl. What would happen to her?

Doctor Gamla came while we were eating our noon meal. She brought a letter from Julius Dahlen, expressing great sadness for Ingrid's death.

"I shouldn't have asked her to travel. It's my fault she took the risk." He had promised to care for them.

"I'll take Alice," Doctor Gamla said. "No use putting it off."

A choking hand clutched my throat. "No," I said. "Mr. Dahlen might take her."

Doctor Gamla shook her head. "No judge would allow a single man to take a girl, especially one feeble minded." She pushed her cheek out with her tongue, smoothing a few wrinkles on her face. "A married man stands better chance of custody."

"The letters from Mrs. Stenson," I said. "They should be worth something." Doctor Gamla agreed to talk to the judge if she saw him in town.

"Will you post another letter?" I said. "It won't take me long to write a note."

"I'll nap," she said. "Riding over creation wears me down. I'm not young anymore."

I was still writing when I heard a commotion in the yard. A man with two small boys drove up in a buckboard with Nickelbo Livery Stable blazed across the side. A coffin wedged beside a trunk in the back. Julius Dahlen.

I took Alice to greet him. He was tall with a face scarred from pimples. He wore overalls and a chambray shirt. Anyone looking at him would know he was a farmer. He wore a black armband of mourning.

"You must be Mr. Dahlen," I said. "I'm Verdie Brandt, and this is Alice."

"Nice to meet you, Mrs. Brandt." His eyes fastened on Alice.

"Please call me Verdie," I said.

"Only if you call me Julius," he said. He knelt down to Alice's level. "Alice, I'm your new daddy."

Alice looked at him without change of expression.

"Can we get down, Pa?" The older boy said. "My butt hurts."

A flush rose in Julius's cheeks. "Harold, we watch our language in front of ladies. Apologize at once."

"Sorry," Harold said. "Come on, Earl."

They climbed out of the wagon and ran toward Doctor Gamla's pony.

"Wait," I said. "That pony bites." Harold disregarded my warning. The pony nipped his arm, causing a howl loud enough to call the fire brigade.

"That's enough," Julius said in measured tones. "That's what you get for not listening."

"Show the boys where the kittens are hiding," I said to Alice. "In the haymow."

She hid her face in my apron as the boys raced toward the haymow, whooping like attacking Indians. Bees buzzed in the hollyhocks growing under the windmill.

Sweat dripped down Julius's face and stained his straw hat. He wiped his neck with a sleeve and shooed a fly. He unhitched the team and led them to the water trough.

The boys screeched from the barn. Julius sighed. "How about it, Alice-girl. Want a pony ride?" He scooped Alice into his arms and galloped like a horse. "Let's find the kittens." He called over his shoulder, "I'll be right back."

Alice showed no alarm as Julius bounced her to the barn. He seemed to be a decent man and a good father, but he was not handsome. Jess's dark eyes and dazzling smile left her dizzy. All the other girls envied her handsome man with his mop of curls.

The horses stomped and swished tails against the flies. They nuzzled icy water, fresh from the well, snorting and splashing like children. I stepped closer to feel the spray of coolness.

Doctor Gamla came outside, rubbing her eyes, and yawning. "Who's here?" She walked over to the wagon and sniffed at the casket. "Needs to go in the ground right away."

Julius returned alone. "Alice is watching the boys swinging on the ropes. They're getting acquainted."

I introduced Doctor Gamla. Her blue eyes bored into him like a search light. "So, you want to take Alice?"

"Yes, Ma'am. I made a promise, and I'm not going back on it," he said.

"You need approval from the judge," Doctor Gamla said.

Julius showed a worried look. "I have letters from Alice's mother agreeing for me to take her in case something happened."

Doctor Gamla shrugged. "First get the coffin in the ground."

"The undertaker costs two dollars," he said with an apologetic shrug. "Can't afford to buy a plot." He wiped his face again. "Decided to take her back on the train with us."

"Hauling a corpse all the way to Jamestown in this heat?" Doctor Gamla said. "There's room here in Verdie's graveyard."

Who did she think she was? Doctor Gamla stuck her big nose in everyone's business. I was about to tell her so when another thought emerged, clear and tempting. If her mother was buried on my land, Alice would come back to visit the grave. A

31

lifelong connection, even though Alice moved away.

Julius removed his hat and slapped a fly. He scratched and jammed the hat back on his head. "I couldn't possibly impose. Mrs. Brandt has done too much already."

"She's right," I said. "There's room."

He dipped his hat in the water trough and poured it over his head. Water dripped down his face and shirt.

"Show him," Doctor Gamla said. "I'll ride herd on the kids."

Leaving Alice with those wild boys might not be a good idea, but the old woman knew a thing or two about children. They'd be safe enough.

We started out for the graveyard. The prairie wind robbed my voice, and neither of us spoke. Fall wildflowers scattered across the hillside, their blossoms blowing until they nearly bent over. The young stock grazed in a fenced pasture. Above, a blue sky, but dark clouds rimmed the western horizon. The outside world invaded my space. I didn't like it.

At the cemetery. I opened the squeaky metal gate. My throat choked and I failed to hide my tears.

"I wanted to ask about your man, and now I know," he said in a low voice. "And losing a baby." His voice caught. "I understand."

I nodded.

"Anyone to help you?"

I shook my head. He didn't need to know about Pa's new wife or how Pa had kicked me out when I protested the marriage.

I recalled his advert in the Montana Matrimonial News. "We are both heartbroken." Our separate griefs reached across the graves and connected us in an almost tangible way. Two strangers mourned tragedies.

"Here." I pointed to a spot by the fence. "But please bring Alice back to visit the grave from time to time." Words popped out of my mouth, unbidden. "Doctor Gamla is always right, even though I hate it."

"She's a wise woman," he said with an easy laugh. "Alice needs to know about her mother. I'll bring her."

We walked to the place where Jess had died, and I told him the whole story. He didn't offer advice.

"It's hard," he said. "Nothing eases the pain."

"Do you ever wonder how the world goes on, though your life is in the manure pile?"

He snapped an Indian paintbrush by its stem. "I thought marrying Ingrid meant the end of my grief."

Back at the house, Doctor Gamla dozed in the shade.

"Oh no." Julius's face showed alarm. "The children."

My heart raced. They might have tangled with the haymow ropes. Anything could happen. We found Alice sitting between the boys with her lap filled with kittens. The boys jabbered a steady stream. Alice looked at each boy as he spoke.

"I knew she'd do better with brothers," Julius said behind me.

"She's beautiful," I said.

We left the children to sit on the porch, sharing a dipper of water. We spoke in low tones to allow the old woman her rest. The team chomped grass beside the barn. The pony dozed in the shade.

"Did you have other responses to your advert?" I said.

"How do you know? Do you take the Matrimonial News?"

"There was a copy in the valise." I felt color rising up my cheeks. "I admired how it was written."

"There were others, but none like Ingrid." Laughter sounded from the barn. "One woman was just released from the work house. Another was a prison guard." He sighed. "Another admitted to lung fever. I have to think of the children."

I shuddered to think of the consequences of a bad choice. I knew what it was to have another woman take a mother's place.

Doctor Gamla stretched and yawned. "There's nothing like a catnap to refresh a person."

She rubbed her eyes. "Did you find a spot?"

"Yes, Mrs. Brandt is very kind," Julius said. "I must dig the grave and fetch a minister."

"I'm going home," she said. "I'll fetch the preacher. He's not much good, but he'll do in a pinch."

The children came running, holding Alice's hands, one on each side. She ran to keep up.

She looked happy. A pang of sadness struck me. Another loss loomed ahead.

"Let's have milk and cookies," I said. The boys cheered and raced toward the house as Julius headed toward the graveyard with a spade over his shoulder.

The minister came by in late afternoon. To my surprise, Doctor Gamla stepped out of the buggy and straightened her back. Introductions were made as Julius herded the children into the buckboard. They needed to have the funeral before dark.

"I thought you were going home," I said to Doctor Gamla as we climbed into the buggy with the preacher.

"Hmph." She glared with such intensity that I had to look away. She had that effect on people. Folks named her a witch because of her herbs and poultices. If I were to think her a witch, it would be because of how she looked right through me. "The judge is gone to Bismarck. Won't be back until tomorrow afternoon."

"What will Julius do?" I doubted he could afford a boarding house.

"I'll chaperone if they can stay here overnight," Doctor Gamla said. "It will give me a chance to get to know him better. Judge Ford owes me a favor for dosing his shingles." She went into a long description of her treatment. "Just like my salve, a little hospitality is a cure for Alice. You don't want her to go to an asylum, do you?"

I wanted to return to wandering the land at night and avoiding folks during the day.

"It's the least you can do," Doctor Gamla said.

We reached the cemetery as the afternoon sun cast a warm

glow over the crosses. Ingrid's grave lay open. Julius wept with Alice in his arms. The boys stood beside him. They deserved better. A sandhill crane settled in a grassy place by the Mad Dog River. If only I could fly away from Jess's death, Alice, and the widow-man. Life was too grim to bear.

The preacher stumbled through his prayers. Doctor Gamla glared at me until I looked away.

"Yes," I said to her in a whisper. "They can stay."

It was only one night. The judge would decide what happened to Alice. It wasn't my business.

"I'll sleep with you and Alice," Doctor Gamla said. "Julius and the boys can have the haymow."

After supper, I drank coffee with Julius on the front step. The evening carried the crisp hint of early autumn. Doctor Gamla and Alice were in bed. The boys played around the water trough, splashing and squealing.

"Do you think Alice knows her mother is gone?" I said.

He heaved a sigh. "It's hard to tell."

He herded the boys to the haymow with a backward glance. "Thank you, Verdie."

I was free to go walking and get away by myself. I wanted to remember Jess's eyes and the soft skin of my baby. I would rest my feet in the Mad Dog River and think. "But I won't go in my nightdress," I said to myself. "Not with menfolk around."

The sun settled behind the western lip of the prairie in ribbons of oranges and reds. By the time I reached the cemetery, the twilight turned to night. A waxing moon showed enough light to illumine the crosses.

I turned my back to the new grave and knelt by Jess's marker. Foolish, I know, but I didn't feel alone. Ingrid heard every word. Ridiculous. I lay my head on the cool ground beside Jess and whispered the day's events. "It happened so fast," I said. "You know how Doctor Gamla bosses."

An owl hooted from the river. I followed the sound to the bank of the Mad Dog. What would I do? I couldn't manage the farm myself and I refused to go back to Wisconsin. Maybe I should read the Montana Matrimonial News. I shuddered. With my luck, I'd end up with a wife- beater.

"Excuse me," a voice spoke in the darkness.

My chest jolted. "You startled me."

"I can't sleep." Julius plopped beside me on the riverbank. "What if the judge won't let me take Alice?" He threw a pebble into the rippling water. "I admit I'm not the best one to raise a girl." He pitched another stone into the river, skipping across the surface in the moonlight. "But I promised her mother."

We sat together on the bank, watching the water flow, the moon rise, the stars pop out until a thousand glittered overhead. A prairie wolf yapped in the distance. A mouse skittered under the dead grass. We were a pair. Heartsick and hopeless.

"I didn't expect Ingrid to love me." He squeezed his eyes tight as if to block out the memory. "It was too soon for both of us."

"Tell me about your wife," I said.

Julius told how they met, and their decision to move west. "I never expected..." his voice quavered, "to lose them both…" He pulled out a handkerchief and blew his nose with a honk. "My sister in Michigan would take the boys, but her man is a brute. I'd starve before giving my boys to them."

"It must be hard," I said.

"We get by," he said with a bitter laugh. "But the boys are on their own too much. I've tried to find a housekeeper, but no woman in her right mind wants to keep house in a soddy."

"Ingrid was willing."

"She would keep house and mind the boys," Julius said. "A marriage of convenience."

"So, your marriage to Ingrid would have been a business arrangement?"

Julius threw another stone into the river with a plop. "At first," he said, "we agreed to see if love grew before we lived as man and wife." An owl swooped and caught the squealing mouse. Julius stood to leave. "Best get back to the boys. Thanks, again."

I watched him leave. I would never love another man, but I could use help with the farm.

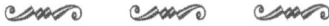

The next day, I tended the boys while Julius and Doctor Gamla went to find the judge.

Alice looked at the boys with bright eyes. They were gentle with her in spite of their wildness.

"Why don't Alice talk?" Harold said. "She don't say nuthin."

"She's thinking," I said. "One day all that thinking will pop right out of her mouth."

I kept an eye on them as I put a pot of beans into the oven for supper. Little Earl came into the house.

"Do you like little boys?" Earl said with a slight lisp in his voice. "We don't got a mother."

He looked so cute with his round cheeks and serious eyes. I knelt down and gave him a hug. "Any woman would be proud to call you son."

He kissed me on the cheek and ran outside. I was smitten. Earl and Harold were sweet boys, boys who deserved a mother. And Alice. She deserved both a mother and father.

The buckboard drove into the yard. By the look on Julius's face, I knew he brought bad news.

"Well?"

"He won't let me have Alice unless I'm married." His shoulders slumped and he twisted his hat in his hands. "She'll end up in an asylum. She don't belong there."

I didn't need Doctor Gamla to give me a cure. "I have an idea," I said. "You come here and work this place. We'll raise these children together."

"Marry me?" He was about as stymied as I had ever seen a man stymied. "Are you serious?"

"A marriage of convenience," I said. "At least for now. But I won't leave my house to live in a soddy. You'll have to sell your property."

"But a lady like you," he said. "Why?"

"A wise man once said, 'We're both heartbroken. Let's join forces and start again.'"

Julius let out a whoop and tossed his hat into the air. The children came running from the hollyhock patch. Harold and Earl held Alice's hands on either side.

"What's wrong?" Harold said.

"Nothing's wrong," Julius said. "I've found a new mother."

"A mother?" they said in unison. "Who is it?"

"Me," I said.

Alice locked eyes with me and smiled. She laughed out loud when I swooped her into my arms. The boys hugged my legs.

Julius beamed. He had the kindest eyes.

## THE END

## *About the Author*

Pequot Lakes author, Candace Simar, likes to imagine how things might have been. Her historical fiction combines her love of history with her Scandinavian heritage. Simar has been recognized by Western Writers of America, Will Rogers Gold Medallion, Midwest Book Awards, Western Fictioneers, Laura Awards for Short Fiction, and the Willa Literary Award in Historical Fiction. Learn more about her work at www. candacesimar.com

# THE DOG STAR

---

### *Harrison Hurst*

Ibrahim ibn Yaqub held up the great white pelt. Thick, dense fur had been cleaned in cold waters to startling purity. Unfolded, it took up nearly the entirety of the table where it lay.

"What manner of monster was this?"

Kåre was clearly pleased with his guest's reaction, though he didn't understand the question. Ibrahim's guide, Trygve, repeated it in Norse, explaining the response in turn. "He says he was trading among the Finns years ago, far to the north. The ship was camped on an icy shore when a bear came down attracted by their food. It took a dozen men to kill it." At this, Kåre poked his finger through a number of holes in the pelt. "He says it would make a poor hanging, but a good blanket or rug."

Ibrahim nodded, attempting to appear politely interested. His enthusiasm made this difficult. "What price?" h8e asked. That much Norse he knew. Likewise, the response. "A quarter pound silver."

Ibrahim blanched. Awe wasn't particularly profitable. He smiled and set the pelt aside. "I would hate to buy your trophy from you."

Kåre grinned, giving as light a reply as his language allowed. "He says you're more than welcome to join them next summer when they sail north again. You can hunt one of your own."

"Cheeky, isn't he?"

Ibrahim drew his host's attention to the chest of raw amber that was his true objective. Pelts were a mere distraction compared to the glittering red gold that the Hedebans brought from the shores of the Baltic. Ibrahim knew better than to ask its provenance as his professional reservation returned. He was genuinely impressed by the bear pelt. He'd seen too many glittering things to be impressed by them anymore. "Ask him if he's considered my offer again."

Kåre barked a laugh, crossed his arms, and shook his head ruefully. Ibrahim hardly needed a translator. But there was a receptive tilt to his head, a considerate gleam in his eye at the rejection. A good merchant spoke well but observed better. Their common language was want and need. This they could exchange without Trygve.

Ibrahim nodded as if conceding Kåre's position. "It's true, you might get a better price later. But I'm here now. Take my money and you can start investing it for the summer. By the time your competitors are out of the market, you'll already be out to sea on the gains of your investment. Admittedly, I don't understand much of your other business—except that time is often of the essence."

Trygve translated this and Kåre was quiet. Finally, he shrugged. "He asks if you can allow him more time to consider. Two days, after the Feast of the Dog Star."

Ibrahim's expression brightened, intrigued. "I think Magdeburg will still be there in two days. We can wait."

Kåre gave a gracious grin and the two men shook hands. "He says you're welcome to join them at the feast. There will be a ritual, a worship service. Afterwards, they give thanks for the star's blessings. It's the God of Plenty," Trygve said, adding his own context, "the God of Prosperity."

"Auspicious," Ibrahim replied. "I'm honored."

Ibrahim and Trygve departed the longhouse, Ibrahim in high spirits. He covered his face with a scarf as they left. Kåre, like other wealthy people, had made use of the courtyard surrounding his home by picketing a slab of meat at the entrance as an offering to the god on the eve of festivities. Given the general poverty of the city, it was a generous offering indeed.

The lands surrounding Hedeby were cold and fallow. Little was grown or raised, more was caught on the open sea; and fish were worth little to anyone but the hungry. Hedeby was advantaged only by its position at the end of the Schlei, an inlet that allowed cargo to be transported from the Treene to the Baltic over corduroy roads, a shorter and safer journey than sailing through the northern straits. Even so, if men like Kåre didn't leave each summer to do what they did—a trade entirely different from Ibrahim's, and one he didn't enjoy associating with the sanguine man with the white bearskin rug—it's unlikely anyone would call Hedeby home at all. They passed more than one slave corral as they walked along the city's wharf, their yards half-empty now, only awaiting the end of summer to fill with human misery. Ibrahim hardly glanced at the vacant stares he sometimes caught peering between the slats of the thrall's barracks.

"We've already made enough here to call our stay profitable," Trygve said. "Perhaps we should leave for Magdeburg while the weather is good, give our condolences for the feast."

Ibrahim looked askance at Trygve, notably dour since leaving Kåre's. "No, I think we can afford two days. Why? Is there a problem?"

Trygve shrugged. "I'm uncomfortable with joining in pagan festivities. I thought you might be as well."

Trygve was more than uncomfortable and Ibrahim sensed it. "You've been acting strange ever since we arrived. Are we in danger?"

"If we were in danger, I would have told you."

"Then what?"

Trygve took a moment to collect his thoughts. "I was raised a Muslim, but my father was converted from idolaters such as these. He told me of some of their rites. They were... incredible. I wasn't sure I believed him, but I've no intention of learning the truth now."

"What rites?"

Trygve hesitated. "Some of man's sins are best left for God alone to know." He gave Ibrahim a look of significance. "I really think we should go. We have enough."

"No, we don't." Ibrahim was a little irritated now. "I risked my life coming here and not for a few dirhams and a handful of stories. I'm going to make the most of it."

Ibrahim could explain himself no further, could not say what he felt; that if there was such a thing as enough—that which was sufficient and secure to reassure him—he hadn't found it yet. Pagans, Jews, Muslims, in this they all agreed that life was bitter and transient, and loss and change were its only constants. In this sense, every moment was the same moment: a question of what you stood to gain and what you stood to lose. No; enough did not exist.

      ❧     ❧     ❧

Ibrahim was half-asleep on their ship when Trygve came to find him. The candle Ibrahim lit cast shadows across a grim expression. "Kåre has sent men. They say the star is bright and the ritual is about to begin."

Ibrahim nodded, throwing on a heavy cloak. He made for the top deck when Trygve took his arm. "The feast isn't till later, after the rites. We can wait here till then. I'll just tell them we're interested in the feasting, not the worship."

"I want to see all of it. I want to know what it's all about."

Trygve looked as if he wished to say more. But he nodded and followed Ibrahim up into the night air.

The two men Kåre had sent were clad in wool and furs, heavily bearded with thick locks of hair cascading down their backs. Their expressions were polite as Ibrahim approached, and with a word of confirmation between them and Trygve, they led the way to the site of the ritual.

The path they took led along the wharf till they reached the naked banks of the inlet on the outskirts of the city. Here, the clusters of small homes and workshops which herded like a flock of disembarked sheep by the water, were quiet with anticipation of the festival to come. Some other figures were headed in the same direction, which Ibrahim soon saw was a solitary pier. Ibrahim noted a reflection of fire muffled by a gathering crowd of worshipers. Looking above their heads, he spotted the star in question, known to him as Al Shira, the brightest star in the sky. Trygve's steps became heavier the closer they came. Ibrahim finally stopped him. "You don't have to go with me. I think I can manage without you until the feast."

Trygve glanced towards the pier, the crowd. "Are you sure?"

"I'll find you afterwards. I can ask any questions I have then."

Trygve was visibly relieved. He nodded and Ibrahim continued on after his escorts. He felt much more alone now and vulnerable, but there was a thrill in the feeling, like swimming out too far into the ocean.

Ibrahim's escorts soon merged with a waiting crowd, dimly lit against the fire they faced, perhaps two hundred people in all. Their faces and features blended together, pale, hairy, speaking softly with one another in guttural tones. Kåre was nowhere to be seen. Granted, Ibrahim struggled to see anything over the leering figures of the mostly masculine crowd. Towards the front of the assembly, he eventually spotted a small group of women, each holding bundles of cloth to their chests. Over the murmur of the crowd, he heard crying from the cloths and realized each woman held a baby, apparently very small, very likely newborn. Ibrahim planted himself where he could watch them unimpeded. The women looked on with somber expressions. They did not speak with one another or anyone else. They did not even stand particularly close to one another. Each appeared to stand alone, surrounded by people.

Beyond them, near the pier, a gothi made preparations for whatever rites were about to occur. He was tall, wearing dun-colored robes and a vestment of dried fish hide that reminded Ibrahim of the tallits of his childhood. His hair was thick and grey, not unlike Kåre's bear pelt in its density, obscuring almost every feature of his face from scrutiny. He worked at a long table like those the Hedebans used for feasting. The table was empty except for a mortar, pestle, and ingredients that the gothi was doling out into the mortar. Ibrahim watched as the man stepped away, and using a pole, retrieved a kettle from the embers of the bonfire. He poured the hot liquid into the mortar and began mixing with short, practiced motions. When he was satisfied, he set the pestle aside and motioned for the women to step forward.

The women set their bundles on the table, some accompanied by men at their side. They stepped back into the crowd, the table now crowded with a half dozen squirming, crying forms, even more discontent now that they were separated from the warmth of their mothers. Ibrahim felt a sinking feeling in his chest, though he couldn't guess what might be about to transpire. Each infant seemed so alone on the table, unable to understand their abandonment, feeling only a present moment of isolation that went on forever.

The gothi moved from infant to infant, taking the mixture from the mortar on his finger and dabbing it within the bundles. The process took several minutes; by the time he reached the last child, the others had fallen silent, though they still squirmed in their swaddling cloths. Ibrahim was struck, and a little disturbed, by this bit of witchcraft. When the gothi had finished, he set the mortar aside and faced his congregation. The crowd was startlingly silent. In his weeks among the people of the North, Ibrahim had never seen them so quiet. All he could hear was the crackling fire and the placid murmur of the sluggish inlet against the shoreline. The gothi began to speak, and though Ibrahim could not understand or follow the service, he understood the tenor of benediction. At one point, the gothi turned and raised his arms to the star above, speaking in a strong voice so that the god might hear them from the earth. He turned back to the table, and murmuring, waved his hand over each infant, coming once more to the end of the table.

The fire had burned lower and the shadows were deeper now about the beach. The congregants were so still it made Ibrahim nervous. He shifted from foot to foot, wishing that whatever was going to happen would happen so the tension in the air might be released. Returning to the head of the table, the gothi took up a bundle, which ceased to squirm as he held it to his chest. He walked away from the crowd, towards the star and the water.

Ibrahim's chest tightened. Truthfully, he hadn't believed Trygve, nor the bitter recriminations heard in childhood against the barbarians who had brought Išbīliya to its knees a generation before his birth. He still felt more paranoid than panicked as the gothi walked to the very edge of the pier, almost out of sight. The Dog Star seemed very far away, like a distant mountain peak above the silhouette of the holy man. He hefted the child away from his chest, presenting it to the star.

There was an awkward thrust. A small shape suspended in air, black against black.

A splash, unmistakable.

When the gothi turned back, his arms were empty. He returned to the table and took up another bundle.

Ibrahim started forward and stopped. No one else moved, no one spoke. He swore, felt weak in the knees, shrunk back from the crowd as if to leave, but his eyes stayed fixed on the procession of the gothi as he made his way back to the pier with another child in hand. He looked to the mothers. Some bowed their heads. Others rested on their husbands. A few looked on resolutely into the night. He felt things were moving too fast, didn't understand how to act, even as each step the gothi took seemed to stretch on with elongated seconds.

Another awkward thrust, another babe sent hurtling into the dark. Another sullen splash, like a large stone.

He was a stranger, far from home, without the rights of home to protect him or to justify his intervention. These were not his children, it was not his God, not his laws, not his people. He felt himself a jinn, powerless upon this plane, but in the next moment was unconvinced of his own impotence as a third child went into the water.

Ibrahim considered leaving. It felt cowardly. He had asked for this, had wanted to see, wanted to know. Now that the moment had arrived, he felt the least he could do was watch, white-eyed, at the demise of lives that would never be. He kept glancing at the crowd as if looking for one sane person who could put an end or explanation to this madness. They remained stoic. More than that, he began to imagine them satisfied. They were coming to the end of a preparatory chore: launching a ship from the beach, laying the foundations of a new home, scaling fish to eat. The death of these children was simply an act of beginning.

It seemed to take hours, but eventually, the table was empty except for one bundle. The gothi took this up and Ibrahim was horrified to find himself wishing it would go quickly, that he would do it quickly. He wanted to retreat to his bunk, wanted to believe he had only fallen asleep and dreamed an evil portent of things to come. He wanted to return to a world where the sacrifice of children was symbolic and provincial, a mere parable for lay people and the peasantry. But the provincial was his—the world had always been such.

There was a terrific wail that shattered the silence. The men around Ibrahim were startled, some reflexively reaching for weapons not at their sides. Halfway down the pier, the gothi turned to see one of the mothers wrench herself from her husband's grasp and stumble forward, clambering for the gothi before she was restrained by her husband and another man. She was screaming, a sob-slick collection of words so simple even Ibrahim understood them. "She has my name! She has my name!" The babe seemed to take up her mother's despair, rising out of its stupor to give a succession of shrieking cries.

The mother was physically picked up, and for a moment, Ibrahim had an image of her being tossed into the inlet after her child. Instead, the two men carried her away from the crowd, till her sobs were lost beyond the firelight.

The child continued to cry as the gothi returned to the pier's end, head bent in an almost comforting gesture to the infant in his arms. Then, with a resolution of final effort, he threw the infant over the side, its pitiful pleas cut short in seconds.

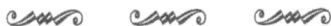

∽ ∽ ∽

There were many more at the feast than the ritual. The night deepened into the early morning. Fires were lit in the city squares so that one walked through shadows into pools of light, with laughing, drinking, and carousing in between. The meat staked outside homes was tossed into these fires so the smell of burning meat was everywhere pervasive. Long tables were set up between braziers as everyone contributed from their own larders. Horsemeat and goat, bilberries and dried apples, flatbreads and pancakes, ciders and meads, and every form of fish conceivable. It was cornucopian, a display of the grace of their god.

A herring stared dull-eyed from its briny soup up at Ibrahim. He stared back resentfully and drank deeply from the beer he'd been given. Trygve watched him with trepidation. The southern merchant had never drunk except to be polite to a host. He was now three cups deep on the strongest beer the Hedebans had to offer, saved only for their festivals. He'd said nothing since coming back from the ritual.

Kåre sat nearby, glancing at Ibrahim with amusement and approval. When there was a lull in conversation with his neighbors, he spoke to Trygve. "He says he's impressed. He didn't think Southerners could drink like Northerners."

Ibrahim found a rueful smile and gave an acknowledging nod to his host. Kåre spoke again. "He asks what you thought of the rites?"

Ibrahim replied to Trygve over the rim of his cup. "Ask him what they meant."

Kåre spoke for a moment. As he did, Trygve's face grew pale. He glanced between Ibrahim and Kåre, sure of what he heard, reticent to speak. "He says the gods hear prayers best with sacrifice. Those families whose houses are full offer their own for the good of all." Kåre looked between the two men and amended, "Girls mostly. At times a malformed male." There was a pause. Bolstered by drink, Kåre elaborated. "Many who have no need of a child leave their newborns in the fens or the woods, but those who give birth close to the ascendency of the Dog Star consider themselves blessed. They send their prayers with the children and the god hears them. The god is pleased and many a poor man has been made rich in this way."

Ibrahim nodded, taking a little too long to respond. Then, muttering, said, "God punished me, bringing me here. I will never forget the screams. You looked into the light of Heaven and found so much want there that you would feed upon your own children. I hope the sea takes you as it took your children. I hope you starve while your god looks on. I hope your star goes out and you are left terrified in the dark."

Trygve's mouth hung open to translate but said nothing. Ibrahim gave a sharp laugh, clapping Trygve on the shoulder, and shook his head. He leaned over the table towards Kåre, his smile fixed.

"The beer, too much," Ibrahim said, piecing together what Norse he could. "I confuse my friend. Want say thank you for hospitable. Ritual was..." He wasn't sure what word to use, feeling above all he should avoid the simple word 'good' as a blasphemy. He ended by raising his open palms with an embarrassed chuckle, unable to say what he wanted. He finally recalled Trygve's word and found it in Norse: "Incredible."

Kåre smiled at the effort and gave a confirmative nod. He spoke and Trygve gathered himself to translate. "He says you honor them. The amber is yours. You may retrieve it in the morning."

Ibrahim bowed his head, dredging up more Norse. "Thank you. Generous. Hospitable. Good food."

At that moment, a song began at the head of the table. It spread down to Kåre, to the men beyond—there were only men here. They sang in the light of their star and Ibrahim was reminded of home: not of the chazzans or muezzins, nor the choirs of the Christians. It was the barking of dogs, the curs of the alleys and their trash heaps. It was the bay of lone and bloody animals, possessing nothing, welcome nowhere, strangers to all but their own company and the secrets of their viciousness. They howled to their star, shining brightly from the velvet dark, a cold eye upon the deeds of men, and they were warm and full and satisfied.

## THE END

## *About the Author*

Harrison Hurst was raised among the mountains and valleys of Tennessee, in the city of Chattanooga, where he earned a dual Bachelor's Degree in History and Liberal Arts. These two fields form the foundation of his work, which seeks patterns in the history of humans and the earth, and elucidates them through art. He currently works as an executive assistant at Walnut Street Publishing.

# WATER-BABIES

*Ann Cwiklinski*

Alice sits on the pantry counter, one eye on the swinging door that conceals her from her parents in the dining room, and snips her hair with her mother's best kitchen shears. When little clumps of light brown hair stick to the sleeves of her woolen cardigan, she blows them off, scattering them like drab confetti across the pantry. Her mother will have to sharpen the shears, and Alice will look ugly for months, but it serves her mother right.

Alice will never, ever stop missing Corinne. But her mother seems to have forgotten the baby already; she and Alice's father have been sitting in the dining room all afternoon, absorbing crackling radio reports about an attack on a harbor called "Pearl," as if nothing else mattered. From her hiding place in the pantry, Alice recognizes the radio announcer's somber, measured voice, but it sounds much deeper than usual, as if he is pushing a heavy lid down on emotions that might try to rise up his throat. She knows how he feels.

Usually, by this time on a Sunday afternoon, Alice's mother is cooking something special for dinner. A roast, maybe, slathered with onions, that slips its delicious aroma under Alice's bedroom door and winding around her nose until she can't concentrate on her library book and has to sneak out to the kitchen to steal a handful of raw green beans to quiet the little growls spiraling up her belly. Or a big, pink corned beef stewing in a huge pot on top of the stove, which doesn't smell nearly so nice, but which draws Alice out to the kitchen anyway, so she can play with the little circles of oil drifting atop the hot water, and corral them with a fork into one big, wobbly circle before shattering it with turnip chunks, like she's a bomber pilot. But today, apparently, her mother has forgotten all about dinner. Even if her mother turns off the radio this second, scoots out to the kitchen, and slams a roast into a pan, dinner will be hours late. And Alice might decide not to eat it anyway, she is so angry about Corinne.

She wasn't going to speak to her mother at all today, but when Alice burst in from Sunday School and dropped her Baby Jesus coloring page on the table, her mother, still in church clothes, clutching her purple velvet hat on her lap, instantly hushed her and leaned closer to the radio.

"What's the matter?" Alice had to ask.

"Something happened to Pearl Harbor," her mother whispered, and hushed her again. Alice thought at first that Pearl Harbor might be the name of a movie star; movie stars were rich and lively and hence prone to automobile accidents. Alice leaned over her mother's shoulder long enough to discern that Pearl Harbor was just a place in the middle of the ocean— though with a name like that, probably a lovely place, a place for mermaids to congregate. When her father explained it was actually a naval base that had been destroyed by Japanese bombers, Alice lost interest. All the radio reports, all the newsreels at the theatre, were about war these days, about far off soldiers in ugly tanks or jiggly planes invading rubbly countries that she knew nothing about.

It was just like her mother to care more about a tragedy far, far away than about a tragedy right here, in Alice's home.

On Friday, Father Doyle took back baby Corinne. Alice's family only got to keep her three weeks. Alice had hoped to adopt her permanently, even though her mother had warned her repeatedly that the baby would have to be returned. Like a library book, Alice had thought, disgusted by her mother's heartlessness. But once, hadn't Alice hidden a beautifully-illustrated library copy of *The Water-Babies* under her mattress, and hadn't her mother searched everywhere, then paid the library fine so Alice got to keep it forever? There would be some way to keep Corinne, too, she'd thought.

It's hard for Alice to believe that it was only three weeks and two days ago that she ran home from school, famished, expecting nothing better than a slice of blueberry pie, and getting the best surprise of her life. As she rounded the corner to her street, she saw her mother on the sidewalk, chatting with Mrs. Connelly from next door. Only when Alice got right up beside them did she notice that her mother held something bundled against her chest. Laundry from the clothesline, maybe? Why would Mrs. Connelly show such a keen interest in laundry? And then…a little pink hand emerged from the bundle and flailed in the air.

Alice gasped. "Ma! Where'd you get that baby!" She squinted at wrinkly old Mrs. Connelly: no, couldn't be hers.

"Father Doyle asked me to watch her a few weeks, until he finds her a permanent home." Alice's mother lowered the baby so Alice could look directly into her staring gray eyes. "Her name's Corinne. She's four months old."

"Ohhhhh." Alice's only sibling, her big brother Richard, was always out playing kickball with his loud friends, and couldn't compare with a baby sister.

"Doesn't her mother want her?"

"Her mother isn't …" Alice's mother glanced at Mrs. Connelly.

"…able to care for her," offered Mrs. Connelly briskly.

"How long can she stay?"

"Only until Father finds her a good home," warned Alice's mother.

"But this is a good home."

"No, you children are growing up; I can't start over with a baby."

"But I can!"

The two ladies laughed.

Corinne turned out be the most adorable, best-tempered baby in the world. Occasionally Alice wondered whether the baby's real mother missed her, whether her heart was broken, but these speculations didn't dampen her enthusiasm for feeding Corinne mush from the sweet silver spoon that had been her own as an infant. She rocked Corinne in the cradle that her mother lugged up from the basement and told her stories about the miserable chimney-sweep, Tom, who toppled into a river and, cleansed of soot and sorrow, became a frolicking water-baby. "But don't you ever run off and get lost," she always cautioned Corinne sternly, as Corrinne hiccupped her tiny laugh. Alice drew pictures of pretty water-babies, blowing bubbles as they darted through seaweed, and stuck them with cellophane tape to the wall beside the cradle, so Corinne could stare at them before she fell asleep.

Alice's mother took decent care of the baby, too, but seemed distracted by all the war news coming from Europe. "How long will this last?" she kept asking Alice's father, as if he knew any better than she did. "Will we get dragged in?" He sighed and shook his head, like he didn't want to talk about it. Alice figured they worried about Richard, who was almost sixteen, and far too foolish to become a soldier. Just two years earlier, he had touched a knitting needle to an electrical outlet to "see what would happen" and been blown across the room. He habitually forgot to do book reports. He couldn't be expected to fight the Nazis with any success.

On the first Friday in December, when Alice got home from school, Corinne was gone, the cradle back in the basement. Her mother pretended it was good news that Father Doyle had fetched the baby to take to her new, adoptive family, who lived miles away. Alice wailed, "I hate you!" and sobbed in her room practically all night. She wasn't punished, which only proved that her mother felt guilty.

And now, two days later, the Japanese attack Pearl Harbor and Alice, angry and ignored, cuts her hair in the pantry. On the radio, the president speaks gravely about "a day which will live in infamy," but Alice hears "...which will live in family." She adopts the phrase to describe her own tragic loss, until Richard teases her.

Alice sulks and her mother worries all week, so early Saturday, Alice's father proposes an excursion. Alice's mother packs a picnic basket and the whole family takes the trolley to the end of the line, to the beach, even though it's December. A few families walk the boardwalk, but the beach is deserted, except for a wind-ruffled seagull down by the water, jabbing aggressively at a crab. Richard jumps off the boardwalk onto the sand and runs into the wind with his arms out, imitating a fighter plane, but with his coat flapping, looking more like a storm-tossed seagull himself. Alice drops herself onto the beach, pulls down the stocking cap that covers her chopped hair, and trudges toward the water. The wind whips her coat around her knees as she stands at the edge of the gray ocean and scans it for water-babies. She could almost swear the waves roar "Cor..." as they rush up to the shore and break, that the whispery foam sighs "...inne" as it slips back to the sea.

Alice's parents hold the picnic basket between them and angle it down the stairs to the sand. Her mother unrolls a blanket and weighs it down with the basket, then joins Alice by the shore. She looks out across the ocean like she's lost something, too.

"Which way is Pearl Harbor?" asks Alice after a long time.

Richard, skipping rocks nearby, jeers, "Don't you know the Atlantic from the Pacific?"

Alice thinks she does, vaguely.

Alice's mother peers intently across the water, as if she can see Pearl Harbor, and the 2000 young men who died on its waves, quite clearly in the wrong ocean. She says, "Their poor mothers."

Oh, thinks Alice: Their mothers. Their wives and sisters and daughters. Those sailors belonged to somebody. A day which will live in family.

For a second, she almost forgives her own mother, and feels a sudden rush of pity for that other mother, the one who gave up Corinne. Even the water-babies, she realizes with a shock, must have once had mothers. A small wave breaks at her feet, nuzzles the tips of her shoes, then swiftly retreats, but as Alice studies the vast, gray ocean, she can't persuade herself it's nearly big enough to wash all the sadness from the world.

## THE END

## *About the Author*

After working as a writer in Washington, DC, Ann Cwiklinski started to write short stories while raising four children in rural Pennsylvania. Her stories have won first prize at *The Baltimore Review*, *CentralPA Magazine*, and local arts events, and have appeared in *pacificREVIEW*, The *Flexible Persona, Belletrist Magazine* (Pushcart nominated), *Crack the Spine, Blackwater Press Short Story Collection 2021, Still Point Arts Quarterly*, and *Minerva Rising*.

# THE BLOOD STONE OF SHIVA

## *A.K. McCutcheon*

Here's what you must know about me: I am a man who indulged my passions for whisky, gambling, and women with generous bank accounts.

And I am a murderer.

Not with my own hands, but a murderer just the same.

There are those who believe it was the stone that killed them. An accursed diamond, the warm red color of blood. As to the truth, perhaps you may judge for yourself. Have a drink with me, mate, and I'll tell you the tale. It was one year ago . . .

New Year's Eve, 1919. Aboard the steamship *RMS Cliveden*, thirteen days out of Bombay, bound for Southampton. The Great War had ended, leading to my discharge from the British Army in India. I had booked passage on the steamer, hoping for a lucky card game to finance my travels.

I was glad to be done with a soldier's life, eager to leave India. I struggled to justify the inequity of British colonial rule. Indian soldiers fought bravely beside us on every battlefront, yet their country was stripped of crops and textiles to supply Britain or sell abroad, reducing the natives to poverty and starvation. Then there came the harsh new laws meant to quash protests and public gatherings. My years reading history at Oxford taught that repression usually leads to rebellion. Indeed, our battalion had seen rioting in the Punjab region. I hoped cooler heads would prevail. I heard talk about protests against the Crown, without violence, led by a native called Gandhi.

On that night aboard the *Cliveden*, there were thousands of miles of deep water between me and India. The sea was restless, as if spoiling for a fight. The passengers—a war-weary assortment of Brits, Turks, Indians, Portuguese—were all on their way to being drunk, or at least the ones who weren't seasick and heaving over the side.

I was in the ship's saloon, at cards with two other fellows: a Sikh, his head swathed in a white turban, and a Turk, his right hand displaying a silver ring in the shape of a wolf's head. The wolf ring reflected lamplight in a manner that dazzled the eye—perhaps a dodgy tactic to distract other players. The mere presence of the Turk was unsettling, as the Ottoman army had opposed us on bloody battlefields just months ago. Even so, cards don't question the nationality of the player. Indeed, disputes between countries might be solved more expeditiously if their leaders would sit down to a gentlemanly game of cards.

Our game needed a fourth player. I spotted a young Englishman at the bar and waved him over. The quickness of his response told me he was no stranger to card play. His erect posture and squared shoulders spoke of military service. I called to him, "I say, were you a fellow trooper? I'm lately with the Royal Fusiliers."

He smiled and shook my hand vigorously. "Jack Shelton. Somerset Light Infantry." He had a bright, cheerful demeanor. I liked him at once.

"Call me Nigel," I said, and offered him the chair nearest to mine at the table.

We fell into our play. The saloon had no windows; the air was warm and heavy with tobacco smoke and liquor. Hours passed. The cards went against me. My watch told me dawn had reached the upper decks when we agreed on one last game. Poker, Five-card draw. Our foreign companions soon folded. It was down to Jack and me. My cards were promising, even exciting, but I had too little money to cover the final bet.

Then I thought: the diamond. I hesitated for agonizing moments—weighing the odds in my favor against the consequences of a loss—then plucked the red gem from my vest and dropped it on the table. Jack raised his eyebrows and smiled. "That will make a pretty bauble for my girl back home."

He showed me a straight flush, spades, queen-high. My mouth went dry. I tossed my losing full house on the table and mopped my forehead as Jack pocketed the red stone with a flourish, clearly relishing his victory. Nausea washed over me, not due to the pitching ship. No soul is more wretched than a gambler abandoned by luck. I'd squandered my fortune, my chance for a future, a home, and a life without a duffel bag on my shoulder.

The Turk and the Sikh said their good-nights and left us. Jack and I took our smokes outside to the creaking deck. We sprawled on wooden chaises, wrapping our coats tightly against the chilled sea air. I raised my voice above the rumble of the waves: "I'll be off when we dock in Port Said. My fare takes me no further, you see."

I glanced at my companion, observing his amiable and trusting manner. How could I bear him ill will for my loss? He had shown himself to be a gentleman. We were fellow countrymen, after all, and brothers in arms. I resolved that we could not part ways until I told him—warned him—of the stone's history. Might he return the gem to me when he learned of its terrible origin? I could only lay out the facts, and let him decide the stone's destiny. "Jack . . . about the diamond . . . there are things you should know.

"Some months ago, our platoon received orders to travel to Amritsar to put down a violent uprising outside a Hindu temple. Before our departure, I overheard a conversation in the company headquarters: two troopers speaking in hushed tones about a statue in the temple. Rumor had it that the statue of the god Shiva the Destroyer was adorned with a red diamond, glaring from its head like a third eye. According to legend, the stone was stained by the blood of those cursed by the vengeful god.

"Was the gem real, or merely myth? A flush of excitement coursed through me. A diamond of that unique color would be worth a fortune. Occupied with my thoughts, I turned to leave . . . and glimpsed the back of an officer's uniform as he made a swift exit from the building. Had he also heard the whispers about the diamond?

"By the time of our arrival in Amritsar, another platoon had engaged the mob and driven them inside the temple. The scene was bedlam: the suffocating scents of incense and gun smoke, the anguished cries of the wounded. Amidst the turmoil, the temple priests hastened to protect the relics. One priest lifted his robes above his knees, climbed to the top of the Shiva statue, and retrieved the red stone. Before his bare feet could reach the temple floor, a bullet dropped him.

"It was our lieutenant who fired the shot. If it was a misfire, or intentional, I couldn't say. As the priest lay slumped beneath the statue, crimson froth bubbling from his chest, he leveled a finger at the lieutenant. Piercing him with a stare like a bayonet, the priest uttered his last words, 'You have angered Shiva. You will appease him with your blood.'

"You might think the priest's curse would have as chilling an effect as the shadow of death, but no, the lieutenant laughed like a man crazed. And then I saw him pry the diamond, wet with blood, from the dead priest's hand. At that moment, I knew the shot was no misfire.

"And here is perhaps the most astonishing part of my story: the lieutenant died that very night, stabbed through the heart in a drunken brawl with a Gurkha soldier in the camp canteen. I witnessed the murder. After the Gurkha fled, I opened the lieutenant's coat and removed the blood-soaked stone from his lifeless body. I confess I felt little shame in doing so, as I had no part in the unfortunate priest's death. If I had not recovered the stone, other hands would have claimed it.

"And now, my good man, the cursed diamond is yours. That is, if you are brave enough, or reckless enough, to risk arousing the wrath of Shiva." I flicked a cigarette butt over the side and waited for a response. Would he react in horror or outrage?

Jack guffawed and slapped his knee. "By Jove, that's a cracking good story. Even if I believed a word of it, I don't hold with fables. It's all the same to me if the stone is worth only a few quid. It will make a memento for my girl in Surrey."

So he was determined to keep the diamond. My hopes for regaining the stone were dashed. I admit the story did seem like fantasy. I lit another cigarette and surveyed the endless blue horizon beyond the railing. "Surrey, you say? My family had a country house in Surrey. I haven't seen home in ten years. Black sheep, you see. I was an adventurer before I joined the army. The family name doesn't sit well on a vagabond who's a gambler to boot."

Jack turned toward me, his expression solemn. "I'm sorry to hear it. If you like, I'm happy to deliver a message to your family. I mean, surely they are anxious to learn how you fared in the war?"

I avoided his eyes. His words affected me deeply, in an unexpected way. I hadn't known any real friends since my school days. My constant travels prevented long-lasting acquaintances, and I was fearful of forming attachments while in uniform—one could never be certain who would live or die from day to day. To think that I would be overcome with gratitude for a few kind words from a stranger . . .

I stood and shook my head. "I appreciate your offer, Jack. But my family lost faith in me long ago. My father made it clear—I have no home there and no hope for it." The sound of my father's voice—decisive, without emotion—still burns in my memory. "So, I'll say goodbye, and wish you safe travels." I offered my hand in parting, and he took it. As it happened, it was not to be our final goodbye.

The *Cliveden* navigated through the Suez Canal and arrived in Egypt that evening. After the engines shuddered to a stop, I shouldered my duffel bag and left my cabin, lurching clumsily as the boat edged toward the dock. I had almost reached the gangway when a commanding voice barked behind me, "Make way! Make way there!" I leaned into the railing as two uniformed ship's stewards jostled past me, straining to balance their shared load—a canvas stretcher, carrying what appeared to be a man's body, draped by a thin blanket. Only his black boots were visible, polished to a shine. Then, as the stewards struggled to maneuver around a corner, a limp hand slid from beneath the blanket, revealing a silver wolf's head ring on the third finger. My bag dropped from my shoulder to the deck as I gaped in disbelief. The Turk. Our card-playing companion. He seemed in perfect health when he left the saloon last night. What could have befallen him?

"Nigel!"

I turned at the sound of the familiar voice. Jack trudged toward me, his face haggard, a deep purple bruise above his brow.

"Jack, what's happened?" He looked unsteady on his feet. I took his arm and led him to a nearby bench at the ship's prow. We sat with our backs to the gangway as the stretcher bearers disembarked with the body.

"That Turkish bloke . . . he must have waited and followed me to my cabin. He crept up behind me and bashed me against the cabin door. When I regained my senses, he was searching my pockets. I kicked at his legs and he fell backward. I heard his skull crack. I'll never forget that awful sound. A steward happened to come into the passageway. He saw everything."

Jack exhaled a long breath. "The captain took my statement for the Maritime Board. He assured me there will be no charges. The steward confirmed my account. And . . . I suppose it's helpful that this is a British ship and the man was an Ottoman Turk." His expression darkened. "His head. There was so much blood. I served my wartime duty in the quartermaster's office. I've . . . I've never killed a man."

I gripped his shoulder. "Jack, the man might have killed you. You acted to save your life. There is no blame there." The bruise on his forehead looked worse on close inspection. "Have you seen the ship's doctor?"

He didn't answer, but said, "He was after the diamond. It was in his hand when he fell. Look—" He pulled the stone from his coat pocket. "Is that . . . is that blood?"

I told him I saw no blood on the gem.

"No, of course, that would be . . . I mean, I don't believe in hocus-pocus and curses." He passed a hand across his face. "I think I will see the doctor. My head is throbbing." He smiled weakly. "So this is goodbye again. Good luck, Nigel."

"Goodbye, Jack. Take care of yourself."

I watched him shuffle away from me until he was lost in the throng of passengers milling about the deck, a sea of khaki and gray and blue. He didn't believe in the Shiva curse, he said. Months ago, I would have said the same. But now—after the lieutenant, and now the Turk—I shivered with foreboding. I hoped that all would be well with my young friend.

I stood and gazed out at the expanse of Port Said. Military and passenger vessels lined the docks, tethered like prisoners in chains. The shouts of dockworkers hovered in the cold night air—unfamiliar languages, babble to my ears. Another new year in another foreign city. Another brief sojourn as a stranger among strangers. There was a time when the novelty intoxicated me. Now there was only tedium and loneliness. I needed to find a card game and a place to lay my head for the night. I hoisted my bag and made my way down the lighted gangway, into the darkness.

Let's have another drink, mate, and I'll proceed with my story . . .

Some months later, at a train station in Istanbul, I came upon an old edition of *The Times* from London crumpled on the floor. The front page headline caught my eye: *General Reginald Dyer Removed from Command*. About bloody time they sacked him, I thought. The Butcher of Amritsar, some called him. I was in Amritsar with my platoon that day. The day I first set eyes on the red diamond. Dyer ordered his troops to fire without warning on a gathering of unarmed civilians in a walled park. Wanted to punish them for the unlawful assembly, he said. Hundreds were massacred. Memories from that day still torment my sleep.

Eager for other news of home, I seated myself in the station foyer and pried open the yellowed pages, determined to read every line. Imagine my surprise to see a familiar name in the society columns. Jack had apparently returned safely to England and reunited with his sweetheart. The newspaper announced the engagement of Mr. Jack Shelton and Miss Arabella Haverly of Surrey, daughter of Mr. George Haverly, deceased, and Mrs. Haverly. *The Times* noted the bride hoped to locate her brother, Alfred, traveling in locales unknown, to escort her at the wedding ceremony in place of their late father.

And what of the diamond, you ask? Ah, you presume there is more to tell, and you are right. Eventually, my travels brought me back to England, and I learned the fate of the stone.

Jack commissioned a London jeweler to set the gem in a pendant necklace as a wedding gift for Arabella. The jeweler confirmed it was indeed an incomparable diamond.

Jack presented the pendant at a luncheon with Arabella and her mother, where he regaled the ladies with the story of Shiva's curse. Both women were horrified by the stone's origin and said they wished they had not heard of it. Arabella declined to wear the necklace and declared that it should be locked away in a jewel box. After protestations and chiding from Jack, she finally agreed to wear it on their honeymoon trip. It was a stunning piece, after all.

On the wedding day, the skies darkened, cracking with thunder and pelting rain. As the happy couple drove to London to begin their honeymoon, Jack's roadster skidded off the slick-ened road and rolled into a ditch. Arabella's neck was broken. She died instantly.

Jack must have ripped the necklace from her throat before dragging himself from the wreck. A passing police constable found him dead, lying in the mud, clutching the pendant. The constable delivered the pendant to Arabella's mother, who packed it away with her daughter's wedding dress.

Arabella's miscreant brother returned from his travels too late to attend the wedding. He arrived to find the bridal couple dead and his mother bereft. Shortly thereafter, his mother collapsed with a sudden heart attack and died three days later. Was it the shock of her daughter's death that killed her, or the sight of me—her worthless son—looming at her door after so many years?

Ah, I beg your pardon, I haven't introduced myself properly. My name is Nigel Haverly. That is, *Alfred* Nigel Haverly. Arabella was my sister, you see.

She was a glorious girl, they tell me. I remember her as a child of twelve years, a beautiful moppet, sporty and lively. She made a game of flinging gumdrops at me to catch in my mouth, laughing the whole time. Happy memories, now sad remembrances.

And Jack . . . Jack was a good man. To think that the card player I befriended on the *Cliveden* would marry my sister and perhaps become like a brother to me . . .

Arabella and Jack didn't deserve their horrible deaths. And my poor mother, always my defender, who begged my father to reverse his judgment against me, to no avail. They were innocent of any crimes. The guilt is mine. I cursed them when I took the stone from the lieutenant's coat. I killed them when I placed the stone on the poker table.

I only wished to acquire the means to escape my wandering life and find a patch of earth to call home. My wish was granted, by the cruelest and most unimaginable means. The home I inherited is now a gloomy country house, rattled by ghosts and echoes. I see their faces and hear their voices each time I close my eyes. And I ask myself: Why was I spared their fate?

As a pitiful penance, I booked passage on this ship to return the stone to its homeland, to its rightful place on the Shiva statue. Perhaps I will bring peace to the caretakers of the temple when I restore the diamond to its home. Perhaps I will find peace in the fulfillment of the task. Or perhaps I must wait to find peace when I rest in my grave.

And so ends my sad tale.

You wish to see the diamond? Well . . . You've been a good sport to listen to my ramblings, so . . . I'll show it to you. I'm careful to keep it close to me, buttoned inside my vest. Here it is . . . Yes, it is a remarkable red color. When I first saw this stone, I saw riches. Now, I see only death.

Well, mate, the hour grows late. We dock in Bombay at dawn. So, I'll say good night. No, I don't care for a game of cards, thanks. I don't play cards any more. You understand, I'm sure. And so, good night.

⌗       ⌗       ⌗

Who's that there? Oh, hello again, mate. You startled me. This is quite an old ship; the passageway is dim. My cabin door has jammed again. It's the sea air, I suspect. I requested a quiet cabin, and as you see, I have the entire corridor to myself. I haven't seen other passengers come this way. Is your own cabin nearby?

Is that . . . a pistol? Why . . . Wait! No!

Ah! I can't . . . get my breath . . . so much blood . . . Stop, stop, keep your hands off me . . . I'll give you the diamond. Here . . . here it is. Take it.

Wait, wait, don't go . . . You have the stone . . . Now, I beg of you, will you do something for me?

I don't want to be buried in foreign soil. Put the pistol in my hands. Tell them you heard the shot and found me dying by my own hand. Tell them I said I want to go home. Do this for me, and you are free from suspicion.

Yes, that's right, put the pistol in my hand. Good, good.

One thing more to tell you . . . You have angered Shiva. You will appease him with . . .

Ah, yes! A quick trigger for such a small pistol. Not so bad to be shot, eh, mate? I did not aim to kill you. No, your wound is not grave. Just lie still . . . lie still.

I will take the diamond from you now.

I hear voices, footsteps . . . They must have heard the gunfire. Our journey will be over soon. We'll be in Bombay soon.

Yes, we'll be in Bombay soon.

## THE END

## *About the Author*

A.K. McCutcheon is a Latina writer and world traveler based in Southern California. She enjoys sending her characters to dark times and places to confront their deepest fears. Her short fiction has appeared in *Elegant Literature*, *On The Premises*, and other literary locales. She lives with her husband in a hilltop home stacked with too many books to read in one lifetime. Connect with her at www.AKMcCutcheon.com

# An End of Troubles

*Hilary Coyne*

**8 February 1587**

Agnes is sure it's a white hart she glimpses as she makes her way up the glen to the castle after a night's leave in the village. There's a bright flash, like the bucking flank of an animal on the run, but rounding the curve of fern-covered rock she sees nothing but a sliver of morning mist twisting among the thick foliage of the glen.

"Just a wisp then." Agnes feels a cold squeeze on her neck as she continues on up the rough path, where the air hangs damp and heavy with the scent of wild garlic. By a dark pool, at the point where two burns flow together in a deep cleft, she finds a curved print in the mud. A hoof mark. Her heart races like a hare through the heather. Riders always take the carriage track to the castle rather than coming up the glen. Drawing her shawl more tightly around her shoulders, she tries not to think about kelpies, those mercurial, malevolent water spirits that the old folk speak of when the minister isn't listening.

During Agnes's climb, a thick grey cloud hangs above the trees, occupying the space where the castle should be. As it clears, the castle tower becomes partially visible, its grey stone emerging as if suspended in the air. A swirl of ice-white vapor has gathered on the rise opposite the castle. It is separate from the cloud around it and, as Agnes looks at it, it resolves into the form of an animal. The creature, a horse in every sense but one, is facing towards a point just beneath the castle wall.

A woman is standing there on the rock they call Knox's pulpit above the chasm cut by the burn below. She wears a black bodice with sleeves of reddish brown and her grey hair is roughly shorn. Her gaze is directed straight ahead, due south across the Devon valley and over the ridge to the silver-grey line of the river Forth on the horizon. The woman's lips move as if in prayer and Agnes sees the rosary clasped at her chest. An unusual sight nowadays.

The cut and fabric of the woman's clothes are those of a lady, the look in her eyes is one of entitlement, nobility, and yet, her hair…Wind shakes the rust-colored bracken on the hillside and Agnes understands; the woman has removed her auburn wig. It must have been more than two decades ago but Agnes knows who she is.

❧ ❧ ❧

The lady had arrived at the castle on a bitter January day to attend the wedding of the Earl's sister. She was twenty-one, a widow, and a Queen.

Forced by the weather to leave the path through the glen, Agnes was hurrying up the cart track when she came upon the Queen's traveling party at the ford just below the castle. Her ladies in waiting were arguing with the Earl's man who had been escorting them up from the village. The Queen's horse had gone lame and in its pained fright had caused another to bolt, overturning the cart carrying her belongings.

The Queen herself was standing apart from the group, back turned, looking up at the stream which seemed to have its source in a dense cloud. Desperate to slip by and get to the castle before anyone noticed she was late, Agnes went too fast over the step-stones in the ford and they clacked together under her foot.

The Queen spun round at the noise.

"You, girl, let us go up!" A flick of her wrist confirmed she meant Agnes to follow.

She had to run to keep up with the Queen's long stride and almost collided with her when she stopped abruptly by the sycamore tree. The Earl had received word of the Queen's arrival and had come out to meet her. He gave a terse bow and turned immediately to usher her into the castle. But the Queen did not move and Agnes watched her take in the dark bulk of the castle tower before waving her over to hold her gloves and crop.

"Welcome to Castle Gloume, your Majesty," Agnes's hand flew to her mouth as she heard her own words. "I mean, Castle Campbell!" It had been renamed by the first Earl over a hundred years before but in the village they still called it by its old name.

The Queen smiled. "An apt name for such a place," she said, glancing at the grey walls of the castle only a few shades darker than the cloud pushing down from the hills above. Her voice was soft and lightly accented with the French she had spoken until her arrival in Scotland just a few years before. She seemed to look past the tower and Agnes couldn't be sure if she had meant the castle or the land beyond.

The Queen turned. "A castle of gloom that sits above a place of sadness. Tell me, do you live in this—how do they call that place? Douleur?"

"In Dollar, your Majesty? Aye. That is, I bide here at the castle but my people are down in the village." The Queen said nothing, raising a hand to halt the Earl who was making his way back from the gate. She seemed to be waiting for Agnes to go on.

Agnes cast about for something more to say. "These burns are known as the Burn of Care and the Burn of Sorrow." The words came in a rush as she gestured to the twin streams running either side of the castle rock. "They were named by a princess who was locked up in the castle for falling in love with a man her father disapproved of. And this is her tree." Agnes placed her hand on the mottled bark of the sycamore. "The 'Maiden's Tree' we call it."

"She was held in the Castle tower?" The Queen's face was both serious and amused.

"Aye, your Majesty. In your rooms. That is, in the ones you'll be staying in for the wedding."

"Well then, I will think upon this princess and her story before I sleep tonight. I fear in this world of men she may simply have exchanged one set of cares for a different one. One sorrow for another." The Queen crossed herself and fingered the small crucifix at her neck.

A vivid image of her own grandmother flashed into Agnes's mind. "Aye," the old woman had said once, taking up her rosary after listening to the tearful complaints of a neighbor, "Marriage is but a beginning, no' an end of troubles."

"I trust we will have dancing tomorrow?" the Queen went on. "Or did your Earl allow the Reformer to sweep away all joy under his great black cloak when he came here building his allegiances against my mother and against me? Against—how did he put it?—the 'monstruous regimen of women'? He had in mind just we three Marias, ruling in these isles, but, with his prejudice to our sex, made an enemy of another who has since become Queen. He might have wished her an ally for his cause but with her fiery hair, she will not easily forgive, I think." She laughed bitterly, one hand touching the russet curls on her own head, and turned at last to the open-mouthed Earl. "Let us go in."

The rest of the Queen's party had now arrived and the royal banner with its twin white unicorns whipped in the breeze as they entered through the Castle gates. As soon as they were out of sight Agnes let out the breath she'd been holding since the Queen's questions about Knox.

A child then, Agnes barely remembered his visit to the castle. Her father had listened to the Preacher give his sermon from the rocky outcrop above the burn. Knox hadn't expected a congregation—"perhaps he was just stoking up the brimstone?", her grandmother had said, eyes flashing—but a small crowd from the castle had gathered below and across from him all the same. That night Agnes's father had told them with a mix of fear and admiration of the words Knox had spoken, the beliefs and certainties he had shared. Beliefs that now formed the heart of their Kirk. Agnes hadn't understood the meaning of it all and, anyway, she always felt there was more of God in the glen and the hills than in the arguments of men.

The day after the Queen's arrival, Agnes was up before most of the rest of the castle. The wedding meant extra work for everyone, and she was to light the fires, empty bedpots and bring water to the guests' chambers. As she tossed the waste outside the castle walls, let out by the watchman who was the only other person up at that hour, she saw someone walking between the twin burns. A white cape gave the figure a spectral glow in the pre-dawn light.

The Queen.

From the mud on the hem of her dress, Agnes knew she must have been walking in the glen. Throwing down the pail, Agnes ran towards her.

"Is everything alright, your Majesty?" Her voice was thin above the roar of the streams. "May I bring you something?"

The Queen turned and looked over Agnes's head towards the top of the castle tower. Agnes curtseyed and as the Queen looked down, she saw a faint spark of recognition in her eyes.

"Ah, Castle Gloume!" she said, turning back to the water. "I thought of your princess a great deal last night as I looked out at her streams du souci et de la tristesse. I have walked down to the point where this care and sorrow flow together. I believe it must be the saddest place in the world. She was punished, imprisoned, for seeking to live as they believed she ought not, yes?"

"Yes M'am...it might just be a legend though—"

"I believe it is not. I sensed her last night in my chamber. A woman who had loved unwisely and naively and was made to suffer for this." The Queen appeared to be thinking about something, her eyes following the separate routes of the two burns as

77

they disappeared among the rocks and bracken of the steep hill. "Although perhaps I was mistaken," she said after a long pause. "Perhaps it was not she in that room but another who will find her misfortune in the hearts of men."

Agnes's tongue found no response to these strange words and she wished herself away from this woman and the intensity that seemed to burn within her.

"Did she die, this princess of the place of sadness?" The Queen's voice was barely audible above the noise of the water.

Agnes's face flared with heat as she realized that she had never considered this. The other stories of the castle were all about men and the princess's tale had become lost under the weight of their legends.

"I…I never heard tell of her end. It's as if she just remained there, locked up forever. But she can't have…" Her voice trailed off in shame at having spoken so much without knowing the answer to the Queen's question. "I'm sorry…I do not know," she managed eventually.

"I shall die." The Queen dismissed the apology with a wave of her small white hand. "Not yet, but before time, and by the will of others."

Agnes felt needle-pricks of panic as the Queen spoke. Surely even to them such words would be called heresy or devilment. Her friends and she had pulled kale and burned nuts on All Hallow's Eve to find out whom they'd marry, but these were mere childish games—kept secret from the Elders all the same. Agnes could not comprehend that the Queen might have foreseen the manner of her own death, less still that she would speak of it.

"Let us walk," said the Queen. "Show me the place where the Reformer spoke. Perhaps I might understand him better. After all, we must, I think, find a way to get along."

Agnes waited, head bowed, as the Queen went ahead towards the castle, her outline blurry and insubstantial in the thin morning light. The watchman clattered to his feet as the

Queen passed through the gate, face stricken with terror at the evident lapse that had allowed her to leave unnoticed. When he saw Agnes, his eyes darkened with both a question and a warning which she could neither answer nor heed. A terse cough from the Queen left him no choice but to allow Agnes on to join her in the courtyard.

There, Agnes pointed to the arched doorway that led into the herb garden and then on down to the flat spit of rock that jutted over the glen to the side of the terrace. The Queen swept quickly past her through the arch and Agnes wondered if she could slip away then, back to the safety of her chores. The Earl had made clear to all at the castle that the Queen was to be treated with courtesy and respect but that they were to keep their distance from her and her people.

A brisk, "Come, girl!" tugged Agnes on in her wake.

At the end of the spit the Queen looked south down the glen and across the valley below. Her body shuddered as with a sudden chill or fearful thought, then she knelt and Agnes saw her draw out prayer beads from within her gown. Agnes's eyes flitted from the empty courtyard to the darkened windows of the tower. If she were to be seen here like this, she'd be beaten. But if Agnes left her there and the Queen complained to her mistress, then she'd be beaten for that as well. She could neither go on nor leave and the pulsing rhythm in her ears drowned out even the rush of water beyond the walls.

At last, the Queen rose and walked back towards the castle, pausing at the herb garden to look to where she had stood earlier between the burns.

"These streams converge," she said, "mixing care and sorrow together. Their progress is unstoppable." She paused and Agnes thought she saw her shoulders sag and a look of defeat cloud her face. "I move against the flow, however. It is harder to do and one is battered by the cares and sorrows both. In this direction the streams eventually diverge. And so, in time, it will be with me and my country."

Agnes considered the passage of the streams down the hill and into the village below and a thought struck her:

"Enough small stones gathered together can change the water's course though, and, given long enough, water eventually cuts through rock. I…I cannot believe that our futures are set." Her voice caught in fear and the words became a whisper.

The Queen stopped and looked directly at Agnes. A smile played across her lips and she drew herself up, confident and powerful. Then, without another word, she moved swiftly across the castle courtyard to enter the door in the tower that led to her rooms.

The marriage of the Earl's sister to the Lord of Doune took place the next day and for the remainder of her stay at the castle, Agnes saw the Queen only from a distance.

Although Knox had visited the castle again in the years that followed, the Queen had never returned. In the turmoil of the decades after her arrival in Scotland, she was, at times, the builder of a dam of tiny stones and at others the rock itself battered and diminished by an unrelenting flow.

When news of the Queen's abdication and imprisonment had reached the village, Agnes had felt a pinch of sorrow for the woman whose life had been steered by forces much greater than herself. The words of her grandmother, echoed by the Queen all those years ago, had come to Agnes then. The Queen had been wedded to men, to her country, and to her faith and all had brought her pain and trouble. And yet, had she not also been the wellspring of others' misfortune, attempting to shape Scotland, 'times against its will, with the force of her nature?

※　　※　　※

The woman on the rock falls abruptly to her knees and leans forward, eyes down as if searching for something dropped into the gorge below. Agnes sees a burst of light above the woman's head, then another, and in that instant the figure—the Queen—disappears. There is a movement to Agnes's left and at the edge of her vision something rises up like a horned animal rearing on its hind legs. She knows that if she turns to look, she will see only mist.

A roar of wind comes down from the hilltop like a beast's bellow of rage and pain. It tears down the glen to where Agnes stands and joins the rushing water of the burn. She follows that cry as it twines with the cares and sorrows of the water and travels on to the Devon and into the Forth before reaching the port at Leith where it meets the memory of a young woman arriving on a troubled sea.

# THE END

**Historical note:**

In January 1563 Mary Queen of Scots visited Castle Campbell – known locally as Castle Gloume – in Dollar, central Scotland, lowland seat of the Earls of Argyll. Seven years earlier the Protestant Reformer, John Knox, had visited the castle.

Mary Queen of Scots was executed in England on 8 February 1587.

## *About the Author*

Hilary Coyne is a Scottish writer of short stories and flash fiction and an independent coach, consultant and facilitator. She was a finalist in the 2023 Edinburgh Short Story Award and longlisted in the Historical Writers Association Short Story Competition. She writes across several genres including contemporary literary, speculative and folklore, and historical fiction. Alongside short fiction she is currently working on a novel centred around an ancient yew tree in 19th century and present day Oxford (England) where she lives. Her published writing can be found via https://www.hilarycoyne.com

# LIBERTY COASTER

## *Sierra Kaag*

Amos crouched down and gave the underbelly of the wagon a hard look, picking absentmindedly at the gravel lodged in his right elbow as he surveyed the damage. The front axle was bent all askew from the impact; upon closer inspection, the weld had also given on one side. The offending curb showed a metallic scratch several inches long. Following one sudden, shaky intake of breath, Amos stood up, pulling at the cuffs of his dungarees, which dangled well above his ankles since his last growth spurt. He scanned the intersection of Cleveland and Minnehaha. It seemed to him as though he must have caused an almighty racket, but the streets all around were deserted, the only sound coming from the rustling of wind in the neat row of maples. He wiped the slickness from his forehead, starting as his hand came away covered in red. Didn't hurt much. Couldn't be too bad. Wouldn't want to worry Mother about it—not this, not on top of everything else. Fishing his handkerchief out of his pocket and scattering several jacks out onto the pavement, he dabbed along his hairline and felt a prickling behind his ears. More blood than he'd thought—was it bad enough to need stitches? Amos had a terror of stitches: last winter Tommy Hadland had sliced his leg after colliding with another skater on Miller's Pond and had to be taken to the doctor, wailing all the way. Amos heard at school that Tommy had kicked the nurse in the teeth when she bent down to clean the wound, and was then pinned to a table screaming bloody murder as the doctor sewed him up. The scar wasn't tidy. Tommy had been showing it off all summer.

Tipping the Liberty Coaster back onto its wheels, Amos gave the black-painted handle an experimental tug. The front wheels refused to turn, tilted in towards each other at an odd angle, but the back rolled along obligingly. Hoisting the metal bar over his shoulder so he could lift and pull more easily, he started off in the direction of the river, dragging his feet in their scuffed and pinching shoes. Without meditating on the why of it, Amos found himself making a beeline for the mute steel works building with its smokeless stacks. Passing along a low brown brick structure to his left, he vaguely recalled a time when he was very small, and his father would come lumbering out of the door in a crush of men after the whistle blew, would then seize Amos and throw him up into the air and catch him with a grin while Mother looked on and tsk-ed in a way that showed she was actually delighted. Turning a corner, Amos's thoughts skipped seamlessly ahead to his father laid out, rendered just barely recognizable by the skill of the somber yet sympathetic undertaker; Mother's breath hitching and catching as she slid slowly down in the chair set at the head of the casket, so that Amos feared she might stop breathing as well.

The move to his grandparents' house over on State Street had not yet taken place, but he could sense its approach by the increasing number of suitcases and crates and hastily-wrapped parcels accumulating in the downstairs hall, and the trickle of neighbors bearing casseroles who then lingered to make tentative offers on pieces of furniture. Yesterday Grandpa Luke, in his come-on-buck-up-now tone of voice, had informed Amos that on the day of the move, he could pack his toys and books into the Liberty Coaster and pull her on over, just ten blocks to the bridge, then another two on the other side of the river, he was a big boy, they'd make their own little parade, how about that? Amos was not fooled. This would be no parade. It was a retreat, a public admission of failure and shame, a delayed cortege accompanied by some grubby belongings. He dreaded the idea of watchful eyes following along as they left the peach-painted house with the closed-in front porch for the last time, and with that humiliation in his mind's eye, it dawned on him that he would now not even be able to play his assigned part in the spectacle. The wagon was broken; he would never have the strength to pull it as he did now once it was filled up with his blocks and roller skates and Dr. Doolittle books and toy soldiers and hobby horse. As his thoughts raced on, his feet slowed. For a few moments he paused, staring at the ground in front of him, doing nothing but blinking, until he realized the cut was dribbling blood into his eye. He wiped his forehead furiously, the renewed sting of it triggering tears. It was that peculiar, desperate sound of an overwrought boy trying to suck sobs back down his throat before they burst out that made Lowell Renquist stick his head out of the door of his workshop.

Renquist's machine shop had somehow managed to keep a toehold while others foundered and sank. Mr. Renquist was known to have a way with stuck gears and recalcitrant drive shafts; the premises were littered with smudged tins of lubricant and scraps of metal that he could somehow coax into being just the right shape and size to fill in for replacement parts customers couldn't afford to mail order. He was also known to fall asleep on the floor of the shop, under the workbench, reeking of moonshine; sometimes in this ignominious state he wet himself. This was why Mrs. Renquist had taken the children and gone to her sister's in St. Cloud. Mr. Renquist didn't seem to mind, or even to notice much. He worked long hours, alone, and for company he had a rebuilt a Marconi radio that was kept on round the clock, even when there was only dead air to play. Occasionally he shushed customers who spoke out of turn, interrupting his favorite broadcasts.

Today Mr. Renquist was mostly sober, it being before noon yet, and he recognized the bloodied kid standing kitty-corner across the street as the Nelson boy. Shame about the father, everyone said. Mr. Renquist's feelings on the matter were neither here nor there, but the radio was playing a cheery Gene Austin tune, and somehow the sight of Amos standing there shuddering in the grip of that powerless, boundless distress we experience only in childhood nudged something in him.

He cleared his throat and called out, "So, didja crash 'er?"

Amos kept his eyes cast down, not trusting himself to speak, not knowing whether Mr. Renquist was the sort of drunk you were allowed to talk to, like Uncle Bill, or the sort you were to avoid like the plague, like the lost men who came and went in waves and often congregated down behind the grain depot. The ones who were to blame for what had happened.

A subtle shift in the set of Amos's shoulders indicated that he had heard, so Mr. Renquist sauntered over, whistling "Yes Sir, That's My Baby" as he bent his big frame at a comical angle to look under the wagon.

"Oh boy. Must've been some bang. Lose any teeth? Or just that scrape on your noggin?"

Amos's dilemma, made even more fraught by the fact that he had been asked two questions at once and could therefore not simply answer "yes" or "no," was solved by shyly baring his teeth to Mr. Renquist, who was able to see that while two were in fact missing, this was old news and not a result of the crash.

"Well, that's all right then. We'll get you cleaned up, then see about that undercarriage." Amos reflexively gripped the handle tight for a split second before relinquishing his hold, numbly drifting after the barrel-chested man into the dimness of the workshop.

Dabbing at his head with a damp rag that had been scrubbed across a piece of carbolic soap, Amos observed the casual way Mr. Renquist flipped the steel body over onto the worktop, pulling and jiggling at the front axle with indelibly oil-blackened and cracked fingers. Amos's eyes widened as one final wrench separated the front mechanism from the body—handle, wheels, axle and all. It was not clear to him whether or not this was part of the plan, and he hiccuped in alarm.

"Not to worry, we'll get 'er straightened out."

The practiced quality of Mr. Renquist's movements was reassuring, and Amos's gaze eventually drifted around the room, spotting a row of five-gallon glass jugs filled with what he now recognized as hooch underneath a shelf piled with odd-looking springs and sprockets. After a few minutes of banging with implements seemingly chosen at random, Mr. Renquist seemed satisfied, striding out the back door with the pieces in his hands, leaving Amos perched uncertainly on the high wooden stool. He heard a pop and a hissing roar—saw the reflection of sparks against the peeling lacquer paint on the door, detected a pungent but familiar smell on the air. Then came a clatter followed immediately by a loud bout of cursing—the wagon's handle had apparently slid down along the wall of its own accord—and then all was still. Amos squirmed on the stool. He wanted badly to see what Mr. Renquist had been doing out back—whether the miracle he was hoping for had in fact been performed— but the echo of a smack upside the head from the last time he had bothered his father in the garden shed reverberated in his memory. He waited.

When Mr. Renquist came in again, he had lit a cigarette, which he clamped in the corner of his mouth while hauling the wagon over the detritus on the floor.

"Maybe not quite good as new, but just about. There you go, son."

Sliding down from his perch, Amos took the offered handle with gusto, tugging it back and forth with all his might. The wheels turned. He tilted the body up. The axle remained firmly attached to the frame. In his moment of surging relief, Amos made the mistake of looking up and meeting Mr. Renquist's eyes. It was the first time he had looked straight at any adult since the body was found. He had been observed by many, his shoulder gripped by a series of concerned hands, but had kept his gaze pointing ever downward.

"Say, didja know my boy? Andy? He's about your age."

Amos blinked. "Class above me." And then, because he had a sense that this was inadequate, he added: "He was nice. But he moved."

Mr. Renquist sucked on his cigarette and nodded. "Sure did."

Amos mustered his most solemn "thank you" and backed out the door, pulling the wagon along with him. He set off in the direction from which he had come, giving a brief, uncertain wave before turning the corner.

Lowell Renquist cleared a corner of his workbench and set out a glass. It was time for the midday news broadcast, so he lumbered over and turned the set down to a whisper before pouring. No point listening to all that doom and gloom, he thought, knocking back the first of what would inevitably become several.

## THE END

## *About the Author*

Sierra Kaag is an American writer and researcher based in northern England. With a keen interest in historical narratives and the personal and cultural significance of objects, her fiction and creative nonfiction explore themes of belonging and the experience of place. Her writing is informed by the years she has spent living and working (and learning and translating) in the United States, Italy, Germany, and the United Kingdom.

# BENEATH HADES' HALLS

### *Harrison Voss*

The steel sliced my father's throat without a sound. His blood sputtered a bit at first, speckling my cheek before hitting the courtyard's flagstones, its scent damp and coppery as our hound Bryas whenever he returned from a stormy hunt, his muzzle slick with slaughter and rain. But unlike Bryas, Father didn't howl. He didn't even gasp. The Spartans holding back his arms had lashed out of him whatever strength he might've used to scream.

But I screamed: to Olympos, to Tartaros, to the Nereids' caverns in the belly of Ocean's deep. It should be me! I roared, not them—give the knife to me! I lunged for the blade only to jolt up in my bed, my palms slick with freezing sweat.

Demetrios stirred at my side. "Hera's tit!" he gasped. He sat up next to me, his eyes wider than a pair of wine bowls at my shouting.

I hugged my knees close to my chest. "Sorry."

"Your father again?" The lad threw an arm around my shoulders, leaning his face close to mine. I crinkled my nose—his breath still stank of last night's eel.

"It's always him."

Demetrios' eyes flashed amber in the dim morning light, his laughter filling up our tent. I almost smiled at the sound of it. "His shade always seems to know when to ready you for a fight."

91

I held his stare. "Do you think we'll battle today?" The question hardly left me when a trumpet cleared the air outside. A flurry of shadows flickered across the canvas, faint and fleeting, as a storm of footsteps shook the earth beneath our pallet. A chorus of heralds' voices lifted in the wind.

"Arm yourselves, Thebans!"

Demetrios chuckled again, brighter this time, melodic as a bell dancing in a shoreline breeze. "The dead don't visit unless they've something to share with us, Kad." He kissed my forehead and leapt out of bed.

We'd been waiting days for Sparta's army to cross the mountains into Boeotia and challenge us. We knew that they would—Thebes had grown strong in her independence, enough even to threaten Sparta's hegemony over Greece. An expedition to snap us into line was inevitable. Once our generals received word of their approach, they commanded us to march out and meet them on the plain at Leuktra, not a day's ride from our city. The Spartan king Kleombratos was a coward by all accounts: half the men thought he'd take his army home once he heard about our march. But the Spartans weren't ones to let shame lie—if Kleombrotos skirted this chance at dominating Thebes, his rule would be remembered as a mockery.

He had to fight. And once we saw the Spartans building their camp on the opposite side of the plain, I knew we would too.

But others were less sure. Our generals debated all day whether to fight or retreat. The Spartans and their allies doubled our numbers. This worried the more conservative generals who held tight to the image of the invincible Spartan warrior, and by the time Demetrios and I went to bed, our leadership still didn't have an answer.

"They must've debated through the night," Demetrios said. He took a sip of unmixed wine from a jug beside our tent's open flap and spat outside.

I went over and did the same. "If so, I hope they're awake

92

enough to lead us."

"I doubt Pelopidas ever rests. Georgios told me he once caught him asleep with his eyes open."

"Didn't Georgios also say he saw a three-armed man win third prize in the last Olympiad?"

Demetrios scratched his beard. The other men mocked him sometimes because he trimmed it, but he never complained. He knew I liked it short. "I didn't say I believed him."

Another set of trumpets roused the morning air, drowning out my laughter.

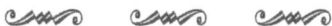

~∽~    ~∽~    ~∽~

Father liked Demetrios before I did.

We first met in my thirteenth year at a funeral for my cousin, Skhedios, whose lover had been Demetrios' older brother. The burial differed from most, for few families in Thebes followed the secret rites of Dionysus as revealed by his prophet, Orpheus, a mortal famed for descending into Hades to rescue his dead wife. We worshipped the same gods and heroes as any Theban did, but reserved our richest sacrifices to Orpheus and the Wine Giver in thanks for their teachings.

Our family hanged a thin bronze tablet around Skhedios' neck before laying him on his pyre. His father inscribed on it the hidden roads Orpheus discovered wandering the house of Hades, guiding mortal shades to what little paradise remained in the land of the dead. I remember wiping my tears against my mother's linen gown, the sound of our weeping drowned out only by Demetrios' brother. But Demetrios stood still, silent, unmoved by his brother's grief.

"That boy has a hero's heart," Father said afterwards. "True andreia." Courage. Manliness. I was envious, but a little impressed too—boys our age rarely had the opportunity to show control over our emotions in front of an audience.

Father introduced us formally after we buried my cousin's remains. "I've seen you race in the gymnasium," Demetrios said.

"You're quicker than any lad I know! You've got to teach me how you ended up with feet like Achilles."

I remember my face growing hot, and being confused by this. I wasn't angry at him. I didn't feel embarrassed. But my legs shook anyways like I'd just finished a hundred stade sprint.

It was the first time I was excited for someone to recognize me.

"I'll look for you next time I'm there," I said. I met him outside the discus yard the next day, and then on the boxing grounds the following. By the time the year ended, not a day had gone by without him.

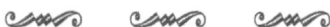

⚬⚬⚬   ⚬⚬⚬   ⚬⚬⚬

Demetrios helped dress me for battle, and I him. Black tunic, white cuirass, bronze helmet. He strapped a thick belt of metal scales around my belly, tightening my linen corselet underneath so that it felt like a second skin.

"Did you know my father asked if I wanted to have his old cuirass before making mine? The whole thing was made of this stuff." He rapped his knuckles against my bronze belt.

"You would've looked richer than Persia's Great King," I said.

"And felt like I was walking in an oven." We both chuckled. Demetrios handed me my spear before taking his shield. He'd painted its outer face with the club of Herakles, son of the god-king Zeus, which served as the insignia of Thebes' Sacred Band. I took my own from its perch against the tent beside his, painted with the same emblem. Our slaves served us our breakfast outside by the fire: barley stew topped with goat cheese, and a cup of watered down wine. We'd barely finished when the heralds made their rounds again, calling for members of the Band to gather in a clearing outside Pelopidas' tent.

Our commander stood on a small platform, though by my memory he didn't need it: he stood a head taller than most men I knew, with a bull's shoulders to match. Between his thundering voice and silver gaze, one would've thought him another of Zeus' mortal progenies.

"I'll keep my words short," he shouted, "since I know none of you need them to kill these bastards." We slammed our shields in answer, howling to the sun. Pelopidas raised his hand, its skin pink as heather in the dawn's rosy light. "You are Thebes' Sacred Band—her three hundred fiercest protectors, her lions. Thebes' generals selected you over all other soldiers because of your devotion to war, to your city—and to the man who stands beside you."

I felt Demetrios' eyes on me before I'd turned to meet them. Both our cheeks flushed.

"Eros will compel you today to protect your lover and excel beyond him. The god will guide your spears and tighten your shields. But only you will be Sparta's executors. Eleven years ago they took the reins of our city against the will of both gods and men. Many men, many women—lovers, wives, brothers, and fathers—were exiled or killed for opposing their rule. Three years later we put our spears together to chase them out of our homes and return Thebes to the hands of her people."

Another shout rose up, louder this time. Pelopidas smiled. "But today the dogs have returned to take back what they think is theirs. To kill more lovers, more wives, more brothers and fathers. Today we remind them that our city, that no city, will taste Spartan oppression again."

The men bellowed, slamming their shields, stabbing their spears into the air, shouting to Eros, to Herakles and Ares, scions of war. Men called our country's plains Ares' dancing ground, where soldiers exchanged skips and twirls for ringing swords and clashing shields. We'll honor the gods with our finest steps, I thought.

My grip tightened around Father's spear.

And they will grant us vengeance.

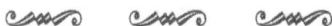

I was fifteen when Father first let me hold his spear. Demetrios and I were boxing in the courtyard in front of my family's home, the evening air hot, our shadows lurching in the dust as he taught me a handful of new swings before squaring up against me.

He raised his hands in front of his face, his leather gloves slick with sweat. Despite having barely a year on me, the gods made Demetrios an arm taller, and thickened his arms to be twice the size of mine. His spat into the dirt between our feet. "Hit me first."

"I don't want to hurt you," I smirked.

Demetrios answered me with a short laugh, and that was all it took to set me loose. I barraged him with a flurry of jabs and hooks, our gloves clapping off one another like whips. My arms began to hurt. I paused, just long enough for him to launch a strike at me. I rolled under it, and drove a short upper cut into his belly.

He stumbled back, panting for breath. "I didn't teach you that." He began to laugh again, only to slip back into a wheeze.

"You did," I smiled. "I watched you hit Orestes the same way in the gymnasium."

Demetrios shook his head grinning. "It still didn't take the bastard down."

Father's applause stole our attention. He stood in the front doorway with his shield resting at his hip and his spear against the doorframe, his hair tied back with a leather thong. The black tresses glistened sleeker than an eel's skin. "You're a fine teacher regardless by the looks of it, Lad."

Demetrios bowed his head. "You honor me, Sir."

Father approached us with his weapons in hand, a ray from the setting sun igniting his shield's gold rim. An image of a jade serpent with garnet eyes flashed in its center—the dragon slain by Kadmos, both my namesake and our city's ancient founder. He set his shield down and held his spear with both hands.

"Has your father let you handle his arms yet, Demetrios?" he asked.

The boy nodded again. "A few times now."

"He's a more generous man than I am." Father thrust his spear out towards me. "Take it."

I did—it was heavier than I expected, especially at its head, though the iron spike at its butt provided enough balance to keep it steady in my hands.

"What do you feel?"

I cocked my head at first, running my hand up and down the weapon's shaft. "Wood—ash, I think."

Demetrios grinned, but Father's face only reddened. "How does it make you feel?"

"I feel…" I didn't feel anything then, except maybe a concern for losing my footing as I found my balance with the spear. "I feel…"

"Power." Father's eyes narrowed to slits, his voice a deep, trembling whisper. He lowered himself to my eye level. "In your hands is the power to take a life, to raze a city. Diomedes, Achilles, heroes like these have wounded gods with such a gift." He reached for his shield and stepped back a pace. "Charge me."

I glanced at Demetrios behind Father's shoulder, his eyes wide as mine. "Father, I don't think that—"

"Charge me, Kadmos!" His shout scattered a nest of thrushes above our front door and my cheeks ran hot as flame. I knew better than to disobey him—the flogging scars that cross-hatched my back were a testament to this. I only wished he'd made this challenge when Demetrios wasn't present—why'd the lad need to see me humiliated?

I slid my hands into a comfortable grip. Lowering the spear to my side, I sprinted forward, clouds of dust rising under my feet. Father kept his shield tight to his front. I stabbed at its serpent's blazing eyes—but the spear only lanced the air. Swift as a falcon, Father sidestepped my lunge and crashed his shield into my left shoulder, sprawling me into the dirt. His spear spun out of sight. My ears were ringing—tears began to well.

"You tricked me!" I wanted to shriek. But he'd knocked

the air from my lungs, and all I could muster was a squeak. I made to stand but Father lurched over me, his spear suddenly in hand, its chill blade pressed against my collarbone. The hair on my neck lifted like hackles.

"Do you understand, Boy?" he asked. "If it isn't your spear then it's someone else's—it's your soul to Hades, your city to crumble." He stabbed the weapon in the ground and yanked me to my feet. "When you have that power, you let it take you. The Spartans took our city because they pounced on us at a time when we'd put our spears aside." His eyes lingered on Demetrios. "Trust this power, Kadmos, just as you should trust your friends who know to do the same." He brushed past me and stormed inside, leaving Demetrios and me to box.

We decided to wash instead. Throwing off our tunics, we doused our torsos with olive oil from a small flask we both carried, taking turns to scrape it off one another with a pair of hooked strigils. Demetrios studied my shoulder. Its skin bloomed black and purple, and scattered a soft blaze down my arm when touched. "My father gave me a similar lesson once," he said. He pointed at a small scar underneath his ribs. "His way of teaching me the importance of the sword. When I complained to my mother, she argued it was his way of showing love." He ran his strigil down my right arm, the bronze hardly tugging its hairs. He knew just how much pressure to use without hurting me.

"The earliest thing I can remember is the bite of his switch." The words burned in my throat. Even before I closed my eyes the vision had rushed over me, soaking my body with the cold, granite smack of a tsunami thrown by Poseidon's hand. He'd tied my wrists to his bedpost, the leather snapping up and down my spine with every breath I took. I couldn't remember what I'd done to deserve this—just as I couldn't figure out why he felt a need to beat me in front of the boy I loved most. "I wish they'd show their love less." I opened my eyes, shivering as they glistened. "Will we live up to them?"

Demetrios took my face into his hands, pressing our

foreheads together. The scent of briny oil fell sharp on my nose. "We'll be greater than them."

The Spartan regime executed Father later that summer, just weeks before Pelopidas led his coup to restore our city's independence. They didn't slit his throat as I later dreamt—the Spartans were smart enough to know they'd only enrage the gods if they slaughtered him like an altar lamb. A craftier execution would satisfy their needs.

They marched Father to Thebes' citadel, placing him on one of the acropolis' high ledges with his hands tied behind his back. At their commander's word, a set of Spartans closed in on him with spears—if he tried to fight them, they'd skewer him, and if he tried to step back, he'd tumble to his doom. His death would be his own choice, not the Spartans', as far as the gods were concerned. In the end I never learned what he decided, for by the time Mother and I reached the agora where his executioners dragged his remains, a pair of vultures had already pecked out half his guts.

The Spartans installed a wooden post beside his corpse with a sign detailing his crimes: Relaying messages to Theban exiles in Athens. Plotting to overthrow the Spartan regime. It was a death sealed by Father's love for his city—a death even I would be happy to one day claim.

For all their savagery, the Spartans allowed us to properly bury him. I suspected it less out of mercy and more to keep our family's anger in check. I knew they'd begin eyeing me more closely. But they'd quickly learn I'd nothing to hide, for Father barred Mother and I from his schemes to protect us in case of a tragedy just like this. His discretion was the only thing I praised him for.

I wanted to love him. What son didn't wish for a father he could admire rather than fear? Hating him only made my duty to avenge him another punishment. But I had to avenge him— it's what the gods demanded of every Greek son, that the rest of Thebes would shame me for if I disobeyed.

I returned to Father's grave the night after his funeral with a black-fleeced ewe. The offering was for the Furies, Night's ruthless daughters. Prayers for retribution belonged to them over any other god. Demetrios came along with a torch in hand, watching as I shrieked and stabbed at my victim's velvet throat, my voice thick with rage. The ewe whimpered a little as her knees buckled and a thin sheet of blood sprayed out over Father's grave, spreading a black pool beneath the moonless sky. It was a good sacrifice by all accounts. I knew the Furies would be pleased.

Demetrios and I sat beside her carcass and watched the cold stars turn. The lad pressed a small token into my hand. "He gave this to me for you," he said. I opened my palm. It was a bronze tablet, just like the one we'd buried Father and my cousin Skhedios with: a roadmap to paradise.

"He gave it to you?" Demetrios wasn't an initiate in our ways, and never showed interest in joining. None of his family believed in our rites, he later explained, even if he may have. He wished to search for them in Hades once he died—being with them was paradise enough.

The lad shrugged, his confusion the same as mine. "I think he knew the Spartans were coming for him. He told me he wanted to be the one to write this for you, so you'd know where to find him."

I closed my palm around the metal. The gods demanded I make Sparta pay for his death, with or without the Furies' help. But what god said I couldn't also exact vengeance against him for all the agony he put me through? "I will make Sparta bleed," I growled. A fire spilled out my chest and poured down my limbs, tightening every muscle. "And once we meet beneath Hades' halls, my father will know I've become his better."

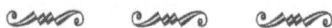

Demetrios kissed me before we filed into the phalanx. He dropped his hand to my waist just as our lips met, his grip tight, purposeful, like a plowman's when seizing the reins of his yoke.

For an instant I swore I could hear the thrum of blood rolling behind his ears. "I've got you," he said. His voice's heavy timber tore a thunderbolt down my spine.

I repeated the same words back at him and watched his smile grow. "Let's go kill some Spartans," I sneered. We marched out of camp with the rest of the Sacred Band, forming ranks along the plain. The Spartan army gathered in the distance, the tips of their spears flashing like stars in the daylight. Thebes' chief general, Epaminondas, deployed the soldiers of our city's allies on our right, and situated the Band directly across from Sparta's hippeis: their king's guard. Rumor had it they could defeat any man in any time, present or past, mortal or deathless. But Epaminondas wouldn't be daunted. He ordered Pelopidas to organize Thebes' soldiers into a spear fifty lines deep and eight men across, with the Sacred Band at its head. Demetrios and I stood in the second line with the rest of the Band's youngest warriors.

Trumpets peeled the air. Our cavalry maneuvered ahead of us into the plain, their whitewashed helmets blazing beneath the midday sun. The enemy's horses rode out to meet them. We marched forward, bellowing hymns to Ares and Herakles, drumming our spears against our shields. Our riders wheeled and jabbed, their javelins cutting through the air. Spartans tumbled from their mounts. Skulls cracked in the dirt. Then another horn went up. This was one of theirs, and their cavalry began to retreat, the hippeis opening up gaps in their lines to allow their horsemen to ride through.

Pelopidas' voice boomed at us from the Band's first line like a slam of Hephaistos' anvil beneath the mountains of Lemnos. A trumpet followed. We charged. Our cavalry darted around our flanks, kicking up reams of dust as they went, screening the Spartans from view.

"Herakles! Herakles!" we roared. We sprang through the dust like shades beneath the earth, ravenous for mortal blood.

Sparta's frontline melted into view, and a wave of panic flooded their faces—they hadn't closed ranks yet from their cavalry's retreat.

Their line crumbled.

I don't remember the face of the first Spartan I killed—only his blood, hot and scarlet, guzzling out his neck. It warmed my skin like a wash of oil after a wrestling bout. Demetrios shouted beside me as he pressed us forward, his spear lancing ribs, cracking shoulders, slicing eyes from their sockets. He sheared the innards out men's bellies with the swift precision of a priest gutting swine at the altar, and the ground quickly started to wreak with just as much shit and blood.

At one point he started to laugh, his voice clearing above the din. "Keep up, Kad! I've seen you dance better before." I howled at the enemy in response, cracking my shield into a Spartan's skull. The man tumbled into the dirt with a shower of blood and brain. "There we go!"

My spear stabbed and recoiled. One Spartan fell, then another, then a third. I roared again, my limbs light. Demetrios did too.

And then I saw him—his helmet's scarlet crest, fanned out like a peacock's plume, was unmistakable. The Spartan king: Kleombrotos. A fresh flame surged beneath my skin. What better prize for my vengeance than the head of a Spartan monarch?

A smug smirk crossed my face. Nothing Father achieved could ever compare with such glory.

I pressed my shield at the back of towering Georgios in front of me. This goaded the lad forward, but the Spartans pitched him onto his heels, their lines tightening the closer we swarmed towards Kleombrotos. Our own lines tightened too.

"Towards their king!" I screamed. Demetrios looked at me, and then in the direction of my spear. He echoed my cry, and amid the roar of clashing bronze and dying men, the rest of our line began to yell: To their king! To their king!

Our lines leaned left towards Kleombrotos, his crest

bobbing closer into view. I forced myself forward, past Demetrios, between Georgios and his lover, into our phalanx's first line. I heard Demetrios shout after me.

I lifted my spear for launch.

A Spartan guardsman flashed his blade in front of my eyes before I could throw it, and my heart went cold. There was a shout, a sudden blur, and a thudding weight against my side. I grinned. His spear missed.

Mine won't.

With a howl to Herakles and Olympos above, I launched my blade into the air, hurtling it towards the pale throat beneath their king's flashing helm. Its huge crest lurched backwards for a moment—and then a hose of blood rocketed skyward in its wake.

The Spartans teetered back. "The King is dead!" someone wailed. "Kleombrotos is dead!"

At the same time, someone keened in our line too: Georgios. "Demetrios, on your feet! Demetrios!" I looked down and my veins froze. Demetrios was curled at my legs, a spear tucked under his left arm, his head limp as a poppy's beaten beneath the rain.

The bastard didn't miss, I thought. I wasn't the target. I dropped to my knees, pulling Demetrios' face to my chest. A trickle of blood creased the chestnut hair on his chin. Our brothers surged forward, enveloping our bodies as they shattered the Spartan line for good and sent the dogs sprinting for their camp, a single word trailing at their heels: "Nikē! Nikē!"

Victory.

꙳　　꙳　　꙳

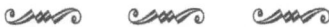

We built the pyres for our fallen at nightfall around the base of our battle trophy. It was a simple thing, as all trophies were: a set of enemy armor held up on a wooden stand. Thebes' generals agreed to dress it with Kleombrotos' suit, his polished headdress hovering over our dead's flames with a comet's gleam.

I laid Demetrios down in his armor with a coin on his tongue. He'd need it, he told me on our last night in Thebes, if he ever wished to cross the River Styx and find his family again.

"My shade will remember you," he'd added. "Even if it cannot be with yours." That night had been endless, amorous—he'd held my body so tight in his bed that even after two days of marching my skin didn't lose the smell of him. He knew our spirits would never again embrace, that only these memories would remain, but they would be enough.

I stared at the metal on his tongue, my fingertips cold as they brushed his sallow cheek and clenched his jaw shut. I pressed our brows together.

His memory alone would never be enough.

Our men started up a dirge around the snapping fires, the thrum of their voices shaking the dirt beneath my feet. I joined them in their circle after setting Demetrios' corpse aflame, Father's bronze tablet, my guide to him and my gloating vengeance, heavy in my palm.

Lifting my face to the blood-soaked plain, I hurled it into the night.

## THE END

## About the Author

Harrison Voss is a native New Yorker. He has published research and essays on the Eastern Roman Empire, Classical Athens, and Roman poetry, and short fiction set in antiquity. When not writing, you can find him running, reading, or scrolling through Twitter.

# THE MIDNIGHT BELLS OF THE ABBEY

## C. T. Bennet

They sent her away for a crime she had not committed.

She thought long and hard before planting the damning details, praying that they would merely be taken as carelessness. The purposely inconspicuous request for herbs that would have delayed her cycle, her new pattern of staring into the distance when she should have been alert, her tendency to jump whenever anyone mentioned the sanctity of marriage.

Finally, the culmination of it all: a slammed door, a hissed intake of breath, a carefully undone dress, a well-paid guard drawing up his hood and fleeing. Which only left Cecily sobbing in front of the man who had supposedly caught her, feigning heartbroken tears.

How was her father supposed to look her betrothed in the eyes, knowing that she willingly sullied herself with a common man? When he had promised that his daughter was the most virtuous in the kingdom?

Later, alone in her room, Cecily smiled, wiping the tears from her face. She did not need to exert any energy to produce them. As soon as her father had invoked King Phillip, and what might happen if he discovered what she had done, the fear that Cecily had harbored since their engagement returned in full force. The prospect of being wedded to such a man, to be his queen and his subject all at once, forced to bear his children until she produced an heir, and the chance that her gambit had failed, dooming her to the marriage anyway—well, it wasn't hard to summon tears and a horrified expression. Her father would see what he wished to see, and he would see a princess who had made a terrible mistake.

"If you are with child, then God help you—" her father had said, once he was summoned to the scene of the supposed crime.

Cecily had shaken her head in response. "I was careful, I swear—"

"Not careful enough."

She didn't protest, not wanting to show her true hand. She was not, of course, with child, nor would she ever be. Her plan made it utterly certain, especially now that she had seen the way her father looked at her. Like she was ruined.

Cecily laid back on her bed, recalling her father's stilted words upon seeing her tears.

"You are to depart in the morning for a convent," he told her. "Be grateful for that mercy. You are to live out your days in seclusion."

It was done. She was free. Free of the court, of her father, of the leers of visiting kings imagining what they would do to her if she belonged to them, of the sword of childbirth hanging over her, the steady monthly reminder that the blood she saw was a harbinger of the blood that would one day soak the child-bed, and perhaps even claim her life.

For once, Cecily slipped into her dreams without trouble, and, for the first time in months, found herself tingling with anticipation for the morning.

She was hurried out of the palace as though the affair she had supposedly carried out was a disease that others might catch. She could bring nothing with her—the sisters of the convent would provide all that she needed, and she was to take a vow of poverty. This was, of course, intended to be a punishment, but she stifled a smile upon learning this.

The journey to the convent was only a few days. The men escorting her did not speak to her—something her father had no doubt ordered. Cecily watched the road in front of her, heart pounding when it became apparent to which convent she was bound for.

The abbess was summoned by the woman who opened the door as soon as she saw the livery of the royal guards, and was given a quick explanation before Cecily was ushered inside the convent.

"Princess Cecily," the abbess said, frowning. "I trust you know what you have done. If you are with child—"

"I am not," Cecily interrupted. "Reverend Mother," she added hastily, at the look upon the abbess' face.

"How can you be certain?"

Cecily hesitated for a moment, but the abbess' eyes implored her to tell the truth.

"My father betrothed to a man who would have treated me like I was not human. If I had asked to come here, he would have denied me. The only way he would have allowed me was if he believed that he had no other choice. I shamed him enough that he could not find a husband for me. The man that I was caught with knew what he was doing. He didn't touch me beyond what was proper."

The abbess did not react as Cecily had feared. She did not tell her to return to court, or even look the slightest bit shocked. "You are not the first woman to have done such a thing," she finally replied. "It only makes it easier that we do not have to worry about a child."

Cecily blinked, hardly believing her luck. "So you are to allow me to stay?"

"If you have come here to seek the Lord and live out your life as his bride and no other's."

Cecily wasn't lying when she nodded. That was why she was here. It simply wasn't the only reason.

Truly, it must have been the Lord smiling down upon her, because after a conversation with the abbess on the layout of the abbey and the schedule that she would be expected to follow, she was taken to the room that she would share with another of the sisters.

As a princess, Cecily had never shared a room, but she did not mind. She would have been forced to, sooner rather than later, and at least now, it would not be with a husband.

"You will share this room with Sister Margaret," the abbess told her. "She is currently cooking the evening meal, and will be your point of introduction into the abbey."

Cecily's heart stopped.

"Is something the matter?" The abbess' voice was sharp.

Cecily shook her head with all too much haste.

"Then come with me to the chapel. You may give thanks for your safe arrival."

Cecily had not lied when she had told the abbess why she had chosen to come to the convent, and so when she knelt in the chapel, and turned her face towards the painted faces of the Blessed Mother and the saints, she was not thinking of the reunion that would come later. When she gave thanks, it was for the chance to live a life of contemplation and devotion, rather than one of servitude and childbearing.

She had never set foot inside this chapel before, but that did not matter. Within moments, it had swept her mind clear of all thoughts but the divine. And she, as always, was overflowing with gratitude for it.

Cecily blended into the shadows during the evening meal, trying her hardest not to look for Margaret, though it made her heart ache. In public, in front of the entire abbey, was not where their reunion should take place. She was determined not to let it be. Margaret did not know she would be coming, after all.

That was, not until the abbess made her way over to a figure that, despite being dressed in a habit like the others, Cecily could identify simply by the way that she stood and the way that she inclined her head towards the abbess.

She whipped her head away as soon as Margaret looked in her direction, and then changed her mind and looked back towards her. The abbess and Margaret stood and made their way towards her, and Cecily's heart, contrary to how it was before, was pounding hard enough that it may as well have been a drum announcing the reason she had prayed that she would be sent to this specific convent.

Cecily caught the end of a hurried conversation between the two women. There was no reason—and no way—to hide that Cecily and Margaret had previously known one another, and Margaret was intelligent enough to say only that and nothing more.

"I see there are no introductions required," the abbess said, her face looking somewhat less severe than it had previously. "I trust you are in good hands, Cecily," she added.

"You came," Margaret murmured, not daring to reach out and touch Cecily.

"Of course I came," Cecily whispered in reply.

It was almost torture waiting through Vespers in the chapel. Almost, but not quite. Cecily let the ritual wash over her, and it worked well enough that she almost forgot who was sitting next to her.

Afterwards, it was all she could do not to run back to their room. As soon as the door was shut, however, the two had embraced, holding onto one another tightly enough that it would have hurt, had the joy of reuniting not been overpowering everything else in the world.

"Was it difficult? Coming here?" Margaret finally asked, pulling back to look Cecily in the eyes.

She shook her head. "No more than I would have expected. My father sent me away almost without thought. And he must have thought of this convent immediately, since—"

"Since that's where my own father sent me." Margaret smiled. "What would they say, do you think, if they knew what they had done?"

"They would exile us all over again."

"Send us to opposite sides of the world, you mean. This isn't exile, Cecily, not with you here."

"I see you've been reading the letters that suitors have sent me."

"The difference is that I mean what I say. They were merely speaking so that they could get you into their bedchambers."

"And where, pray tell, are we right now?"

A laugh bubbled out of Margaret, and Cecily could have cried from sheer happiness. This was why she had risked her father's wrath, and prayed to be sent to this convent. This was why she had cried herself to sleep for days at a time after Margaret was sent away. The sound of her laugh, the glimmer in her eyes, the way she looked as though she had been brought back to life.

"Cecily, I have to know. Who was it? Did you—"

"Edmund Bywater. He did not touch me. I gave him a pouch of gold, and he told me that he had been linked to a man in town, and that he needed to leave. He lives close to the border, so he told me that he would flee. He'll seek favor from the king; it's rumored that he... has several favorite courtiers. Men who are very close to him."

Margaret let out a breath. "Please don't be angry, Cecily, that I asked."

She shook her head. "How could I? You were not there, so how could you know? But I love you, Margaret. Nothing will change that. If I failed in my plan, I would have wasted away in the tower of King Philip's castle, thinking of you and hoping to find you in heaven one day."

"Now who's thinking of the letters the suitors sent you?"

Cecily buried her head in Margaret's shoulder, breathing in the sharp smell of the incense on her habit mixed with the warm, heady scent of Margaret herself. "I missed you."

The beds that they had been given were arranged against opposite walls. They spent an hour lying in the one that had been saved for Cecily, a slim candle on the stand, speaking of the dreams that had come to fruition and the dreams that they still kept in their hearts. Of life at the abbey and the left-behind life of the court, and how they would never be forced into it again.

When the candle burned down to a waxen puddle, Cecily and Margaret stood and sank into the opposite bed. Now both would bear the imprint of a person, and no one would have to wonder why the blankets of Cecily's bed had not been disturbed.

The bells tolled in the abbey as Cecily and Margaret wrapped their arms around one another and let their eyes flutter shut. Cecily found herself asleep immediately, lulled by Margaret's soft embrace and the steady beat of her heart echoing in her ear.

She would have endured the tears and the rage over and over again, as long as it meant that this was how she could fall asleep, night after night. Far above, the moon made its silent sweep of the sky, and the bells tolled again. It was midnight in the abbey, and there were two women desperately, hopelessly, consumed by love.

## THE END

## *About the Author*

C.T. Bennet is a writer and college student studying creative writing, classical humanities, religious studies, and medieval studies. A lifelong literary enthusiast, she is fascinated by history and mythology, and writes a combination of mythology retellings, fantasy, and historical fiction. Her time spent reading and translating ancient Greek often makes it into her writing. She has been telling stories since before she learned to write, and can often be found with a book in hand.

# WHEN THINGS COLLAPSE

## *Anna L. Deh*

I heard a gunshot. From my hiding spot in the front yard, behind the fencing and next to the bushes. Then there was yelling, of something happening that I couldn't see. I saw Alexander coming down the road. He kicked down the door, breaking into his own house.

I heard a gunshot.

The sound bounced off everything around me. It rattled the tulips and the ground itself. Within one second, I knew exactly what had happened. But still, I wanted to believe everything would be okay. I got up and looked through the closest window, the one in the front garden. It was open.

I saw Lydia on the floor, her body still. My grandmother. Gone.

I heard a gunshot.

Alexander stood over her body, phone in hand. He was speaking quickly, the adrenaline still coursing through his vindictive veins.

Alexander turned his head; he saw me through the window.

"Yes. I have a girl I'd like for you to collect," he paused. He spoke slowly and with profound clarity. He wanted me to hear each syllable, to witness the choice he'd made for me. He believed in the loneliness of an orphanage, having lived it himself, he knew how that abandonment ate away at goodness and purity. In his eyes, it was a worse fate than if he had turned the gun on me.

Without another thought, I started to run. I wouldn't have more than a few minutes before the van would show up, ready to carry me away.

Then I ran.

And ran.

And ran.

❧       ❧       ❧

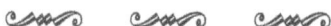

The months had passed. The August heat had cooled, turning brisk then quickly freezing over. Still, the city winters somehow felt colder than the ones in Tver. It might have been something to do with the way everyone had kept to themselves. In cities, there would be no neighbors coming by to check on you, no strangers smiling at you as you walked. There came a point when I too joined the somber frowning faces in the crowd, not making eye contact with strangers on the metro or letting other people know the thoughts behind my empty eyes.

Even though it was a common sight, this seeming emptiness, it had grown over these four months. I felt it when I stepped outside to the grocery store, or simply walked down the street. There was a pervasive silence that no one wanted to break.

The normal rituals were in place. Buckwheat porridge boiled on the stove. Olga had made too much again and it was on the verge of spilling over. She was stirring the pot, her wrinkled hands diligent, mixing the plain goop as best she could to avoid any unfavorable clumps. Over the months I've come to know her, she struck me as a strong woman. She was the only one I knew who lived alone, without a husband or even a boyfriend she could have easily plucked from the street, with her soft tan skin and bright green eyes that only wrinkled when she was concentrating too hard.

And she didn't seem to mind it, this solace. I never saw her cry or look less than content. But at the same time, she never shared much of her past with me. We lived in this state of equilibrium. That I was another person she had to care for, and she did it so naturally.

The wind was blowing in through the curtains, their lacy trim matching the tablecloth. There was so much that matched in the kitchen, yet looked out of place. The tablecloth was a bit yellow at the edges, the curtains a little blackened from the city pollution that bled into the home. Olga kept the kitchen as pristine as she could, but there were parts where her busy hands had missed, the bits of flour on the counter, the newspaper clippings she had failed to put back in the drawer. All the little signs of disorder that added up to something bigger.

Olga slammed the wooden spoon down on the counter, splattering oats against the wall. "Did you see the paper? The one from today?" she asked as she turned around, her eyes lit up with what I could tell was worry.

I reached for the newspaper on the table, brushing off the bits of food and other questionable messes I couldn't quite place. My eyes skimmed the headline:

*Soviet Union Collapses: Gorbachev Submits to Yeltsin*

They called it Perestroika. A reform. I furrowed my brow, unsure but just as anxious. I had heard the rumors. They were impossible to ignore. You could hear it in the whispers in the grocery store, scanning the full shelves that no one had any rubles for. They stayed stocked for days until the bread would blacken with mold, the cheese curdled. Trash cans overflowed with what could have fed many.

Olga and I looked at each other, my hands still gripping the paper. I dropped it as if it was hot, dangerous. It likely could be.

"What do you think we should do?" I asked.

"Eat. That's already hard enough." Olga plopped some breakfast into her bowl and took the seat across from me.

I stared at the headline, feeling the words crowd my brain, unable to grasp the meaning or the wavelengths it might send our way. It didn't feel right to just read the words and do nothing.

There were pictures under the words, with people who looked like they were on the brink of something. Their mouths wide open, shouting against the backdrop of the Kremlin. I wondered how it would feel, to write exactly what I felt on a piece of paper and storm the world with my thoughts and misgivings. What kind of woman would I be then? Would I be someone powerful? Brave?

"Maybe we should do something," I voiced, dropping the newspaper back on the table. Small gusts of wind blew the pages back and forth, flashing the headlines like a fluorescent warning sign. I looked out the window, barely seeing any people out and about. A mix of winter chill and the looming sense of chaos.

Olga didn't respond, she only scooped her food into her mouth. The porridge was mushy—there was too much water in it—to make it last longer. She was messy about it, almost as if someone would barge in through the doors and take it away from her.

She gulped her tea down with the same ferocity, and I wondered how it didn't scald her throat. "It'll pass. All things do."

She sounded so much like Lydia.

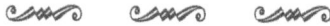

❦   ❦   ❦

The cold air bit at my skin, I could feel my cheeks reddening. Before Perestroika, these walks were merely an escape. There wasn't much of a destination to them and little reason. But now it was a part of my essential routine, like cleaning my body with hot water or waking up. If you didn't get to the bread line, and if you didn't do so early enough, you would be out of luck for the day. And enough of those kinds of days, of those mistakes, could be the difference between starvation and survival.

My worn boots felt cold from the leather that was beginning to thin and tear. It was still early in the morning, the darkness confirmed that it wasn't even 6 a.m. yet. I saw another woman up ahead. Her scrunched body and slow pace, coupled with the scarf around her head labeled her a babushka.

Is this what Lydia would look like if she had been given another twenty years? Would she have been this woman, hobbling into a hungry, desperate crowd? I could see some pieces of her gray hair, peeking out from under her scarf and the too-thin yet overbearing coat she had thrown over her body, dragging bits of the thin wool along the dirty snow. If too much of the snow hit her body, I was worried she might become buried in it, that the elements would weigh her down. She already struggled to move her body against the wind, of all the ways life had gotten in her way.

I couldn't imagine Lydia becoming this way, of fragility and time blocking her path. But I also would never get to imagine it, of all the ways her life had been lost to circumstances. I had seen the beginning of the graying of her hair, of the wrinkles and sun spots, but she wouldn't get to blossom further because Alexander had destroyed the hands of time. It was cruel to see Lydia's future lost, of the ways she could have settled into her age, like the way someone would settle into a comfortable couch, their bones aching and tired. It's impossible to know what she could have become.

But somehow, the babushka in front of me had prevailed. She had done something right to get here, in front of me, breathing in the same cool December air, the kind Lydia would never have again.

Then I did something strange, bad even. I walked faster. My boots slammed against the concrete, and I heard the intensity of my boots against the snow. It was only amplified by the silence and the slowness of the babushka. I was gaining on her, her coat and fabric becoming more apparent to me now, more dingy and sad with every step I took. I realized, suddenly, that I hated this woman. Her presence was a reminder of our fates, how some got to live and others didn't. Maybe she had a daughter, or a son, or a granddaughter, that loved her more. Ones that took care of her better, protected her. Or she was smarter than Lydia had been. That she had chosen a better man to marry. One that wouldn't kill her.

I felt my body grow hot under my coat, and my legs blaze. If I were a bull I would have knocked her down. When I blazed by her, the force and speed of my body made her trip. I acted stupid, but I knew that my shoulder had hit her.

I didn't stop and I didn't apologize. I had heard the soft woosh of air that escaped from her mouth as she fell, when the air momentarily left her body and she fell over. I could hear her hitting the ground, the snow seemingly doing little to cushion her fall.

I didn't stop. I kept on in the same rushed, frantic state. I would be one step, one body, closer to the front of the line and maybe I needed this more—a chance to live. Because I now felt like I was living, symbolically, for two people. And sometimes one had to be ruthless to get ahead. If Lydia would have adopted that idea more, if she had pushed people out of the way, she might have made it.

I had made it farther down the street now and I made myself stop. I turned around, squinting my eyes to adjust to the breaking dawn. The old woman was no longer there. I had left her behind. I wondered why she didn't yell at me or scorn my lack of respect. She had taken the fall like someone would take a minor inconvenience of the day. But I was at fault. I had caused it and I felt—well that was the problem actually, I didn't feel much of anything.

I kept walking, slowing my pace now that the urgency and the adrenaline had cooled in my veins. And I was almost there now, I could see the edge of the line here on Tverskaya Street, against the backdrop of polished marble and elaborate arches that we would be waiting under, gathering like hungry, cold sheep.

There were more people today. News had likely spread about this location, hidden in a nook of the street, right next to an unassuming tailor shop in the middle of this narrow alley-way. One thing Russians did very well was spread vital news to those we cared about, and the news spread like a web, collecting all of us here. I took my spot behind a man with pronounced sideburns and what I could only assume was his wife, who wore a black hat that sat too tight against her scalp.

The man had an arrogance to him I didn't like. It was something about the eagerness in his eyes, how he looked like he would push people aside at any moment. Maybe that was a feeling that lingered in me as well, having done just the same and in a much more brutal way. I shook my head at the thought I could be anything like such a desperate character.

His wife had a coldness to her too, but it was hard to say if it was simply because she knew the brutalities of her husband or if she simply wanted to look like she didn't know him. There was a rule of one bread loaf per household. There were special, assigned Men who were supposed to check for such things at the front of the line, but they were just as tired and worn down as the rest of us and let carelessness take over. But some days The Men came in blazing, their eyes lit up with the disbelief of the crumbling Soviets, hanging on to communism like a lifeline, that if they let rules and order slide, then they just might perish too.

So the wife was gambling. She stood a few feet away from her husband, her wedding band shining even in the winter gloom. I noticed just how much it matched that of the husband. I would have made for a good officer, if I had been born a man and if I actually believed in the regime, if I could spout the idea of brotherhood and of the common good the ways they did, pouring out of them like a fountain.

"Can you see anything?" the wife whispered, daring to get a little closer. She got on her tiptoes, making her still look comically small.

"No. The line isn't moving," he whispered, not turning around.

She paused and let out an exasperated sigh, clutching her lower abdomen. "I don't know how much longer I can stand."

"There's no other choice. The other lines nearby have no doubt filled for miles. We commit to this one," the husband said, growing agitated in his tone. He was so direct with his words, no softness or compassion for his ailing wife.

The wife sat down on the icy concrete sidewalk. I remembered the old wives' tale of how women shouldn't sit down on cold floors, especially concrete since it could lead to infertility. What were the complications if a pregnant woman sat down on it? Would it lead to an automatic miscarriage?

"You can lean against me if you want," I said, unsure where such an offer came from. Was it guilt from what I did earlier, finally bubbling out of me? Did I feel that I had to make up for my bad action with a good one? Like I was evening out my karma, hoping it would pay off and I could get a piece of bread.

The wife looked up at me as if she didn't understand what I had just said.

"You shouldn't sit down on the cold floor."

The wife laughed. "Did your mom tell you that one too?"

"My grandmother."

She adjusted herself, crossing her legs as she leaned against the wall behind us. She looked comfortable now as she settled herself. "You can't believe everything your grandma tells you."

Another half an hour had passed and we were all still in the same place, stuck and rooted without any other option. There was this feeling of unrest in the crowd, I could feel it with the way we all looked at each other, frustrated that they wouldn't do something about the stalemate. But really, we were upset with ourselves, for our lack of power or control over the situation. I thought about leaving, surrendering for the day. No one would have to know. I could just tell Olga that they ran out of bread or that it wasn't safe anymore, that people had grown violent.

Almost as soon as I had the thought, I noticed shouting from up ahead. It sounded like a woman. "Help! We need help!" She kept shouting over and over, with a sense of panic and helplessness that only women could properly mix together and vocalize.

I moved my head, trying to find an angle in the crowd that had now broken the line formation, spreading across the street like ants when they sensed danger and order no longer mattered.

People were pushing forward, deciding that they no longer cared for rules. Persistent mothers and scared children moved in unison with the men who had nothing to lose and no family to care for. It felt like being in a tidal wave, the force so powerful that I couldn't break from the crowd.

I didn't fight back against the crowd, the man from behind me pushed me and I didn't resist. My cheek pressed against the wife's coat, and I don't think she had noticed, so focused she was on the spectacle before us.

That's when it all started to come into view, but not fully. The edges felt blurred, my brain failing to grasp the picture as a whole.

There were two men standing in the middle of the circled crowd, like roosters in a fighting ring. The bundled people looked like they were ready to place their bets, wondering if one of them would die. Or maybe they would both simply kill each other, leaving two more pieces of bread up for the rest of us. Everyone's eyes had lost the desire or urgency in helping people see reason.

Now, there was only hunger.

One of the men lunged forward, tackling the other. A few men in the crowd cheered, waving their fists in the air and shouting as they did so. It had all become surreal.

The men rolled around on the ground, taking turns toppling the other. Punches and shouts became the only sounds. Some women gripped their children tighter, others covered their children's eyes.

The first time I'd seen blood, the type brought on by violence or rage, was when I was six.

It was late morning and my tea had cooled on the table. I had orchestrated a reenactment of a TV show I saw the other day—The Land Before Time. I didn't have any boy toys like dinosaurs, so I used the dolls I had. One was missing a leg but I thought it made the story seem more wild—more true to life. For a couple of hours, I lived blissfully in my imagination.

But then I put down my dolls and I noticed the quiet. Which I remember finding strange; there was always someone's voice or their actions, breaking the silence somewhere.

I thought back to what Lydia said that morning, about her going to the market. How she would look for the cream Chupa Chups for me. That she wouldn't be gone long. Alexander was likely upstairs in his office, drunk and impaired. At this realization that I was alone and unsupervised, I felt a slight rush of adrenaline, the way kids do when the first touch of mischief grasps their minds and limbs.

I tiptoed into the kitchen, keeping my ears alert for the turn of the lock in the door as I grabbed a stool to climb. I knew there was a liter of Coca-Cola on the top of the cabinet, reserved for special occasions. Well, today I ordained that it was special because it was my half birthday. Or close to it at least. The excuses rushed through my head, popping as quickly into my childish mind as the drink dripped down my mouth, sugar and fizz invigorating my senses.

I drank it all. The mix of caffeine from the Coke and knowing that no excuse could save me now made me feel restless. I had lost control and would pay the price. I grabbed the now empty plastic bottle and chucked it out the kitchen window, trying to hide the evidence. I still don't know how far I threw it, only that it was never found again.

Guilty and worried over the punishment I would undoubtedly face, I ran out of the kitchen and down the hall to my room. I closed the door and hid under the blanket, thinking that if I looked distraught enough, guilty enough, then I could somehow run away from the repercussions.

The quiet broke. It was suddenly replaced by the mixing of two voices: Lydia and Alexander. I heard them, but I stayed hidden, living within my shame.

"You forgot the liquor." It was Alexander's voice, emerging from wherever he came out of.

"Good. You don't need more of it," Lydia responded, and I was surprised that I couldn't hear any hesitation. All of her bottled emotions leaked into a few words.

A quick moment of silence, then the sound of skin tearing, of bones snapping.

Then the yelling. Lydia's voice tore through the house the way her skin had torn at Alexander's punch. I could hear the footsteps getting louder, closer to where I had hid myself.

I dared to peek from under my blanket. Lydia ran into the room, her head tipped backwards as she tried to control the bleeding. Her eyes drifted somewhere between being lost and completely aware. They would lose focus, unsure of what had just happened, then they would snap back like a rubber band. It was strange to see, as if her mind was at war with herself, slowly piecing things together but then losing them again.

But Lydia looked in my direction and she snapped out of her haze. She became pure focus. "Alona, give me your blanket." I didn't know how she could see me. I thought that I had vanished and I couldn't be found. Those were the rules. I was off somewhere I couldn't be found.

"Alona!"

Then the blanket was off me. Lydia had grabbed it, leaving me bare and exposed. I had returned to reality against my will.

Lydia used my blanket to soak up the blood. Lydia had told me how she had to do this for Mama when she was alive, how she would coo and shush Mama's cries until they softened. She reserved these rare moments of softness for when they were truly needed. My heart ached for the mother I didn't know and how much Alexander hurt her too. And for Lydia, who watched it happen in a repeating cycle.

Up until he killed her.

I continued watching Lydia. I thought of how much they were alike—Lydia and Mama. Like they were two people fused together into one. I thought about going over to Lydia, joining her. But all I could do was stand there, afraid and cold without my blanket. I was sad that the hiding was over. That the high was over, that the crash was here.

But I remembered a feeling of ease as well.

No one asked about the Coke bottle.

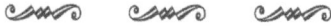

                            

The gunshot startled me.

The crowds didn't start screaming. Not right away. No one started running frantically, as I would have expected. I couldn't tell if the people didn't want to lose their spots, or if we were all numb already, so much so that we couldn't gauge a gunshot as a threat, but a mere suggestion.

An officer pointed a gun in the air. He seemed so tall, that his arm hovered high above us all, governing us. Or trying to. I looked closer and saw that he was standing on a wooden box. What a cheater, I thought.

He waved the gun in the air. "Order! If one more person fights or shouts, then there will be no more bread."

Then another gunshot. I watched the officer, ready for him to shoot another, the bullet lost somewhere in the air.

But the officer dropped his gun and grabbed his chest, which had a clean hole right above his heart. He toppled over, his feet hitting the stupid box. The crowd had entered into a sort of war cry, storming the area in a way that reminded me of Victory Day parades, only more primal. The screams felt like war cries as the people tackled the other officers, who weren't so totalitarian anymore. A couple officers tried to fight back, reaching for their guns. But they were torn apart before they could pull the trigger. The ones with any sense just started throwing bread into the crowd.

Bodies pressed against me from every corner. I was somewhere in the dead center of the chaos. It was the feeling of being trapped and caught up in a moment bigger than yourself. I managed to get on my knees, crawling through the crowd as quickly as I could without getting trampled. Until I could find a way out.

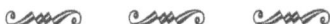

It was four o'clock and it was getting dark. I would be heading back home without a loaf of bread to account for, as if I had failed and dawdled around all day. Maybe I could say that I gave my bread away to an orphan. But Alexander was an orphan so I had long ago lost the belief that orphans were all good, all innocent and sacred. I knew I wouldn't give them something of my own, not willingly.

I had a couple more blocks to come up with a story for Olga and Dimitri. Should I cry? Too bad tears didn't have much power anymore. People cried too much, there was always too much emotion sputtering out of everyone.

The streets were largely deserted. People were likely at home, watching Gorbachev lose his power, at long last ushering in something new in Yeltsin's hands. Those still out on the streets were doing so for two reasons: for causing trouble, or none at all. They were as aimless and lost as our nation. I didn't know which group I fell into yet.

Keeping my head down and my hood on, I walked down the street. My legs were quick, I didn't want to look like I didn't know where I was headed. I was only a few blocks away from the apartment before I heard a man's voice.

"Dochka, where are you going?" he said, leaning against one of the buildings on the street. He had a pale face, his features ashen with smoke, likely from a coal factory nearby. There was something about his expression, almost as if he was sneering at me. It was when he took out a piece of bread from his pocket and shoved it into his mouth, exposing the decay from his teeth that I knew why he made me feel this way. This strange, grotesque man had something I wanted. Something that I had failed to get. Somehow, he was better than me.

I didn't respond, and I had quickened my pace, getting closer to the man but knowing that if I simply kept my body at this pace, that he would come and go. That he would soon be behind me. There were only a few more steps I had to take before I passed him.

But he grabbed my arm just as I was about to put him behind me. "I can give you a loaf. A whole loaf, back in my room." He pointed upwards, his eyes grazing over my body, as if he could somehow tell what I looked like under the heavy coat and heavier coating of fear. "I have a soft spot for orphans."

I don't know what disgusted me more, this man and what exactly he was implying, or how I momentarily considered it. How I could just close my eyes and let the man do whatever he wanted for a few minutes. Then I could go home, a whole loaf in hand, and pretend that the earlier events never happened. It would be yet another secret I could keep.

But going along with this would mean admitting to something I could never make peace with, more so than handing my body over as currency. It would mean that Alexander and I were similar. That we both navigated this world alone, without family ties to guide us. I could never see us as having anything in common, no matter how true. I had to be better than him because I had known love from Lydia, something he never had. Even if it was now lost to me, I wasn't an orphan in the emotional sense. I would forever cling to the love I knew.

"I'm no orphan," I told the man, who sunk his shoulders and swallowed the remainder of his bread, quickly biting into another loaf that he removed from his coat pocket. He chewed loudly, with his mouth open in an exaggerated manner. His saliva coated the bread in a way I could only describe as violent, something beyond plain hunger. Anger perhaps? Yet I was unsure where the feeling was being placed, at me or at the state of the world around us. Maybe he was angry that even in such trying, hungry times, he still couldn't make a deal with a desperate woman, that he couldn't trick her into submission.

I tried not to run the rest of the way home. I kept my pace even. Controlled. Because that's what I wanted to be even if the world was working against me. That even during the collapse of the world around us, I would be a stone pillar. Strong and controlled.

## THE END

## ***About the Author***

Anna Deh received her MFA from The University of San Francisco, where she also worked as a Fiction Editor for *Invisible City*. She resides in the Bay Area and is currently at work on a novel.

# Acknowledgments

Publishing an anthology involves the efforts of many talented and creative individuals. From the moment our authors began writing to the moment you hold this book, years of hard work and coordination have gone into creating this enjoyable and enlightening collection of stories. In short, many people contributed to making this a great book.

Let's start with our authors. This anthology began as a short story contest. Thank you to all the writers who submitted their stories. Creating and submitting a story requires vulnerability. Thank you for being vulnerable and sharing your stories with us.

To the ten authors featured in this anthology, thank you for sharing your stories with us and allowing us to share them with our audience. You have created wonderful masterpieces that inspire, inform, and entertain. Your work is truly invaluable.

To our twenty-three contest judges, all I can say is WOW! Thank you for your time and talents. Thank you for sharing valuable insights with our writers and helping us evaluate all 126 submissions. We couldn't have done this without you. Our judges include: Rachelle Kuehl, Grace Turton, Anika Feinsilver, Tala Kim, Ian Tan, Nalina Cherr, Violet McCann, J. E. Weiner, Elizabeth R. Andersen, Carl Maronich, Colin Mustful, Bex Roden, Diana Giovinazzo, Stephanie Landsem, Jill George, Jillian Forsberg, Edie Cay, Alina Adams, Robin Henry, Eric Z. Weintraub, A.M. Symes, K.M. Butler, and Jenny Quinlan.

To our cover designer, Mel Nigro, and our interior layout designer, Inanna Arthen, thank you! You made the design process easy and created a beautifully designed book that exceeds all expectations. I cannot thank you enough.

And finally, to you, dear reader. Thank you. What good is a book if there is no one to read it? You are the heart and soul of every book we publish. Thank you for keeping great literature alive and for giving us—the writers and creators—a space to be vulnerable, a space to be ourselves.

# ABOUT HISTORY THROUGH FICTION

History Through Fiction is an independent press publishing high quality fiction that is rooted in accurate and detailed historical research. As publishers of historical fiction, we seek to provide readers with compelling narratives that also act as valuable historical resources. Our books, though fictionalized, include important primary and secondary source materials that are disclosed to readers through a variety of traditionally nonfiction elements such as footnotes, endnotes, or a bibliography. This way, readers may enjoy a fictional narrative while also examining the historical foundation upon which that narrative is based. By combining elements of fiction and nonfiction, our authors provide readers with an immersive experience that is both entertaining and educational.

If you enjoyed this anthology, please consider leaving a review. It's the best way to support us and our authors. Plus, you'll be helping other readers discover this great collection of stories.

Thank you!

**www.HistoryThroughFiction.com**

9 781963 452167